"I wasn't sure if I should call to tell you this," Tia began, "but—" She paused. "Okay. Here it is— Conner called me. He's home. And he'll be at school tomorrow."

Elizabeth blinked. She bit her lip, not realizing that several seconds had passed without her responding.

"Liz? You okay?"

"What? Oh, yeah, yes. I'm fine," she said, standing up and grabbing at the edge of her loose-fitting pink T-shirt, suddenly needing to do something—anything— with her hands. "It just took me a minute to—"

"I'm sorry," Tia broke in. "I shouldn't have called. I didn't mean to get you upset. I just wanted you to be prepared."

"No, I know," Elizabeth said. She held a hand to her chest and closed her eyes, trying to calm herself down. "It's fine. *I'm* fine. Really. Thanks."

"Yeah?" Tia asked, sounding unsure.

No. Not at all.

Don't miss any of the books in SWEET VALLEY HIGH
SENIOR YEAR, an exciting series from Bantam Books!

Visit the Official Sweet Valley Web Site on the Internet at:

www.sweetvalley.com

Francine Pascal's
SVH **senior**year

Meant To Be

CREATED BY
FRANCINE PASCAL

BANTAM BOOKS
NEW YORK · TORONTO · LONDON · SYDNEY · AUCKLAND

RL: 6, AGES 012 AND UP

MEANT TO BE

A Bantam Book / April 2001

Sweet Valley High® is a registered trademark of Francine Pascal.
Conceived by Francine Pascal.
Cover photography by Michael Segal.

Produced by 17th Street Productions,
an Alloy Online, Inc. company.
33 West 17th Street
New York, NY 10011.

ISBN: 0-553-49344-2

Visit us on the Web! www.randomhouse.com/teens

Published simultaneously in the United States and Canada

Bantam Books is an imprint of Random House Children's Books, a
division of Random House, Inc. BANTAM BOOKS and the rooster
colophon are registered trademarks of Random House, Inc. Bantam Books,
1540 Broadway, New York, New York 10036.

PRINTED IN THE UNITED STATES OF AMERICA

OPM   0 9 8 7 6 5 4 3 2 1

To Nicole Pascal Johansson

Ken Matthews

I like things to be black and white. Yes or no. That's why I've been going crazy during this philosophy unit in history class. All we do is talk about questions with no definite answers.

Until this karma thing came up—now, that's a type of philosophy I can deal with. In fact, I'm going to start to apply it to my own life. It's pretty simple—you just put out there what you want to come back to you. You know, treat others how you'd like to be treated, that sort of thing.

Um . . . I wonder if there's any way to fix what happened in the past, though. Because I just dumped Melissa.

And I do <u>not</u> want that coming back my way.

Conner McDermott

In my "support group" yesterday we talked about toxic relationships and realizing your potential and cosmic forces—all of that Oprah-speak type stuff. Whatever. All I know is if there's any truth to that karma thing, I have a lot of bad things coming my way.

melissa Fox

I can't believe we wasted an entire history class last week talking about karma. Karma is a bunch of bull. <u>You</u>—not some unseen magical thing—control what happens in your life. And you're seriously deluded if you don't get that.

For example, the fact that Ken broke up with me is not some punishment for what happened between me and Will. It just happened.

But I can tell you one thing—Ken is going to be sorry.

CHAPTER 1
One Step at a Time

"What's more pathetic?" Tia Ramirez asked Andy Marsden, pulling her oversized white V-necked T-shirt over her crossed legs. She and Andy sat side by side on her four-poster bed, numbly staring at the TV set across from them. "The fact that couples actually go on this show? Or the fact that we're sitting here on a Saturday afternoon watching it?"

Andy ran a hand through his red hair, his eyes glued to the television. The show was called *Test Your Love*, and at the moment a stiff-looking, blond-haired guy who was trying *very* hard to appear hip (read: baggy, straight-out-of-the-catalog clothes and a leather-strip necklace) was introducing three couples, all of whom had perfect hair and perfect bodies. Perfect, that was, in the southern-California sense—meaning artificial and unoriginal. Since this marked the third episode in a row that they had watched (it was a *Test Your Love* marathon), Andy knew that in the next half hour these couples would

1

answer pointless questions and laugh at Kip Carson's (Mr. Wanna-be Hip's) corny jokes along the way. Whichever couple ended up with the most correct answers would be proclaimed the winner and would win a "dream vacation" to either Las Vegas or Hawaii, at which point they'd jump up and down, kiss, and dance along to the beyond horrible *Test Your Love* theme song.

Still, as lame as these couples seemed with their overly enthusiastic giggles and over-the-top kissing and cuddling, Andy could come to only one conclusion as he realized that he and Tia hadn't moved off her bed in the past hour. He let out a sigh.

"That we're watching it," Andy said, reaching into the value-size bag of BBQ potato chips that sat in front of him. "Definitely." He crunched down onto a couple of chips. "No question."

"Really?" Tia's dark eyebrows arched in concern, her brown eyes opening wide. "You think?"

"Yes." Andy gave her a mock-solemn nod, patting her narrow wrist. "I'm afraid so."

Her shoulders slumping, Tia glanced back at the TV as Cynthia, the curly-haired female counterpart to couple number two, guessed what sort of scent "drove her boyfriend wild."

"Oh God." Tia brought both of her hands up to her face, then dramatically fell all the way back onto the bed, her long, dark brown hair splaying across her white pillow. "Andy! How did we become so . . . *boring?*"

Andy glanced over his shoulder at Tia as the show broke for a commercial. "Gee, thanks. I can always count on you to boost my self-esteem."

Tia rolled her eyes, pulling herself back up to a sitting position. "You know what I mean. Not that *we're* boring, but our lives totally are." Her full lips formed into a tiny frown. "How did that happen?"

Andy shrugged. "It's a true mystery, Tee." The show came back on, and Andy slid off the bed. He needed to take a break from this before his brain turned to *total* mush. "I'm gonna get something to drink. Want anything?"

"No." Tia sighed. She rested her chin in her hands. "I'll stay right here—and be pathetic."

Andy smiled and shook his head as he walked out of Tia's bedroom and into the hallway. Tia was the biggest drama queen he knew. The girl was the *king* of drama queens. Still, as Andy stepped into the darkened kitchen and remembered that he and Tia were the only ones in the house (even Tia's little brother had somewhere better to be), he realized that Tia *did* have a point. Andy reached up and grabbed a glass from the cabinet next to the sink, thinking about the fact that his social calendar hadn't exactly been bursting lately.

But you can't accuse me of having a boring *life.* Andy opened the fridge and helped himself to a two-liter bottle of soda, pouring some into his glass. It wasn't that long ago that Andy had come to the overwhelming realization that he was gay *and* had come out to his friends and family. That alone had kept him mighty occupied for the past several weeks.

Okay, it *was* fair to say that Andy's love life had been somewhat stagnant, well, forever. But that was because Andy didn't really know how to deal. It wasn't like there were tons of other out-of-the-closet teens strolling around Sweet Valley. Dale, his friend Rebecca's cousin, was the first one he'd met—and the guy was cool, but there wasn't really a spark. Besides, even if Andy did find a connection with someone, he wasn't sure if he was ready for a relationship. Just the thought of it sapped all the moisture out of Andy's mouth.

Oh, well. Andy put the plastic bottle back in the fridge and picked up his glass, heading back down the long, narrow hallway toward Tia's room. *Guess I'll just have to deal with* Test Your Love *marathons for now.* But one thing was certain. He *had* to pull Tia out of her depths of despair. If Andy needed drama, he'd watch the soaps. It was downright painful to hang out with Tia when she got like this.

4

"Andy, oh my God, you missed it!"

Andy blinked as he walked back into Tia's bedroom. Was this the same girl who was wallowing in self-pity moments before? Tia was now bouncing up and down on her bed, her mouth broken into a signature smile that lit up her entire face.

Andy placed his glass down on Tia's dresser. "I want one of whatever you took."

Tia laughed, hopping off the bed. She walked over and squeezed Andy's arm, her big eyes full of enthusiasm. "Listen to this: *Test Your Love* is going to be doing a high-school week. They're looking for teen couples that have been together for six months or longer, and Alcon Studios in Big Mesa is one of the recruiting spots—that's like ten minutes from here! *And* the winning couple will win a trip to New York to the station's headquarters!"

Tia grabbed Andy's glass off the bureau and downed the remainder of his soda.

"And this relates to us because . . . ?" Andy asked, frowning.

"*Because,*" Tia responded, placing the glass back down. "We can pretend to be a couple and try out for the show."

Andy scrunched his red-blond eyebrows together. He really wished Tia would start making sense because he was beginning to get worried. No,

5

he *was* worried. "*Pretend* to be a couple? Why would we want to do that?"

Tia shrugged. "Well, for one thing, we'd kick butt. No couple knows each other better than we do, right?"

"Maybe, except that we're *not* a couple and—"

"And if we won, we'd get to go to New York," Tia continued, pulling herself up onto her desk.

Andy closed his mouth. He *had* always wanted to go to New York City. He stuck his hands in the front pockets of his carpenter pants and glanced at the TV. It was the end of the show, and the winning couple was doing their crazy victory dance with Kip Carson.

Andy looked back at Tia. "But if we did this, we'd be one of *those* couples."

"No," Tia argued, pulling her legs up onto the desk. "We'd just be *with* those couples. We'd be much cooler. And that's only if we win. If we don't, it's just a day's entertainment."

"Yeah, but . . ." Here he'd finally collected the guts to come out to his friends and family and he was going to "play straight" as Tia's boyfriend?

"Andy," Tia said, shooting him a level stare. "Think about it. What would you rather do tomorrow? Go to a TV studio and try out for a game show with the possibility of winning a trip to New York or sit around here with me?"

Andy's shoulders dropped. "So how long have we been together?" he asked.

Elizabeth Wakefield sat down at her desk on Saturday afternoon, fully intending to complete her creative-writing assignment, which was only one part of the hours of homework she had ahead of her this weekend. The problem was, the moment Elizabeth typed the date on the computer screen in front of her, she was struck with a paralyzing realization—Conner was really coming home soon.

Pushing a strand of her shoulder-length blond hair behind her ear, Elizabeth grabbed her date book out of her backpack and flipped back a couple of pages to double-check. *There.* She bit her lip, twirling her heart-shaped necklace around her finger. Elizabeth had marked the day Conner went into rehab. Okay, fine. She knew it was slightly dorky to make a point of noting every event in her calendar, but she couldn't help it. And there it was, *Conner gone*—in red ink. It had been just about six weeks—which was how long the program was supposed to last. And last night Megan had confirmed that he was coming back any day now.

Elizabeth glanced up at her computer screen and stared at the cursor, which seemed to be blinking at the same rate that her heart was now beating. She lifted a shaky hand to begin typing, but there was no way she could write now. She felt drained of any creative energy. And when Elizabeth thought about how she had first met Conner *in* creative writing . . .

Elizabeth stood, wrapping her gray hooded sweatshirt closer to her body. This was pointless. She needed a distraction. Then she'd get Conner out of her brain and get back to work. Hopefully.

Elizabeth wandered out of her room, heading for her twin sister's across the hall. Jessica was always good for a diversion. But as Elizabeth pushed open Jessica's already slightly ajar door, she could hear Jade Wu talking.

"I think it's kind of cool that he has his own weird sense of style," Jade was saying as she flopped belly down on Jessica's bed. "At least he doesn't look like a carbon copy of all the other preppy guys in Sweet Valley."

Jessica, who was sitting in her swiveling desk chair across the room, hugged her knees to her chest. "Mmmm. So now that you've found Evan, you're dissing guys like Jeremy?"

Elizabeth's stomach dropped. She knew she shouldn't be jealous of Jade and Evan . . . and she wasn't. Really. After all, Elizabeth was certain that she and Evan should only be friends—that their kiss had been nothing but a mistake. Still, it had been weird to see

8

Jade and Evan together at the game last night . . . and to hear Jade go on about him now. It felt like it had all happened a little . . . *fast*.

Elizabeth took another step into the room and forced a smile. "Hey, guys."

Jade sat up. "Hi, Liz."

Jessica swiveled her chair all the way around so that she was looking right at her sister. She dropped her feet to the floor, her red-painted toes wiggling on the carpet. "I thought you were going to do nothing but work today."

"That's what I thought too." Elizabeth sighed. She walked over and sat down on the edge of Jessica's bed, playing with the smooth edge of the comforter. "But I'm totally out of it."

"Serves you right for trying to work on a Saturday," Jade commented as she lazily wrapped a strand of her dark hair around her finger. "Saturdays are for playing."

Jessica let out a little laugh. "Yeah, right. That's *Liz* you're talking to." She picked a pack of Trident up off her desk and unwrapped a piece, popping it into her mouth. "So, what's wrong?" she asked Elizabeth.

Elizabeth stared back at her twin. This mental-telepathy thing between them was sometimes a little too much. "What do you mean?"

9

Jessica shrugged as she tossed the gum wrapper into the garbage can under her desk. "Just that you're usually only out of it when something's wrong. And you're looking kind of pale."

"I am?" Elizabeth asked, her shoulders slumping. Why did she always have to look exactly like she felt?

Jessica nodded.

"Definitely," Jade added.

"So, what's up?" Jessica prodded.

Elizabeth bit her lip. The truth was she didn't even want to *think* about Conner at the moment, much less talk about him. But she also knew that her sister wouldn't let up on her. Besides, maybe it would be good to say it aloud, to put it out there. . . .

"It's just that Conner's coming home soon—I think."

"He called you?" Jade asked, scooting closer to Elizabeth on the bed.

Elizabeth's cheeks flushed. "No, nothing like that. But Tia and Megan told me he's going to be back."

"Wow. Are you freaked out?" Jessica asked. She watched Elizabeth with a careful expression, her blue-green eyes serious. "I mean, do you want to see him?"

Elizabeth stared blankly at her twin. That was the million-dollar question, wasn't it? Did she *want* to see Conner? A few weeks ago Elizabeth would have thought she would be able to immediately answer no. But now . . . well, now Elizabeth was realizing it wasn't all that black and white. Then again, nothing with Conner ever was, was it?

She attempted a casual shrug, pulling her legs up onto the bed Indian style. "I don't know," she responded quietly. "I really have no idea how I feel."

But that wasn't the total truth. Because while Elizabeth didn't know exactly how she felt, she did know that at the moment, she was feeling *a lot*. Tons. More than she should, considering how Conner had acted before he left.

Elizabeth swallowed. When it came down to it, she was feeling much more than she could handle.

Conner McDermott was sure of one thing as he tossed an old gray T-shirt into his navy blue duffel bag on Saturday night—he never wanted to step into this room again. Conner hated this suffocating, tiny bedroom, with the off-white walls, industrial tan carpeting, and musty, damp smell that Conner could never get rid of, no matter how much he left his small, rectangular window open. Not to mention the paper-thin walls and the freak who stayed upstairs from Conner, always making random bumping noises in the middle of the night.

Conner was *not* going to miss this room.

11

But that was about the only thing Conner was sure of. When it came to every other question, he only had a bunch of contradictory answers. Was he ready to check out of here tomorrow? Yes. Was he ready to go home? He wasn't too sure about that one.

Conner threw some socks into his bag and then dropped down onto the springy bed, rubbing the back of his neck to try to release some tension. Okay, yeah, Conner was more than ready to get on with his life and deal. He did actually feel like he'd learned a lot in this place, and he knew he could move forward from here. He really did.

But when he thought about having to face everybody after—after knowing he'd been more than a jerk . . . when he thought about having to see them . . . see Elizabeth . . .

Conner stood. He pulled a mound of boxers out of the open wooden drawer by his bed and threw them into the bag. The thing was, he *wanted* to see Elizabeth. He'd thought about her plenty—too much, probably—while he'd been here. When Conner considered the reality of it, though—the concrete moment of having to look right into Elizabeth's eyes and explain . . . Conner let out a deep sigh. How was he going to do that?

But as he zipped up his duffel and tossed it onto the floor, Conner remembered what Jeff, his counselor, was always telling him: "One step at a time, man. Just take it one step at a time." As much as Jeff had totally annoyed Conner, he knew the guy was right. First, Conner had to just concentrate on leaving here. Then he'd deal with facing everyone at home. That was step number two.

Conner walked over to the window and stared out at the gray, overcast sky. It smelled like rain. Then again, it always smelled like rain in this room.

The messed-up thing was that step number one—leaving here—was more complicated than it should have been. Conner wasn't just leaving this place. He was leaving a *person*. Conner glanced over at the enormous oak tree on the far side of the lawn, its weighty branches rustling in the wind.

That tree always made Conner think of her. And when he walked out of here tomorrow, he'd be leaving that tree—and her—behind, forever.

TIA RAMIREZ

Teen Look Magazine
Quiz: How Well Do You Know Your Guy?
Do you have any clue what makes your boyfriend tick? Take our quiz and find out!

1. Your guy's perfect Sunday consists of:
a) Watching football on TV with his buddies.
b) I'm not sure. But he seems to like to go shopping with me.
c) I don't know. We don't usually talk on Sundays.
D) NONE OF THE ABOVE!

2. Your boyfriend's birthday's coming up, and you want to score with an awesome gift. You:
a) Brainstorm a bunch of ideas, then survey his friends to see which idea is the best.
b) Have known for weeks what he wants. You pay attention to these things.
c) Give up and ask him what he wants.

OKAY. ENOUGH WITH THIS INSANE QUIZ. I'LL MAKE UP MY OWN!

Andy Marsden

ANDY: ANSWER THESE QUESTIONS AS BEST YOU CAN. WE'LL GO OVER THEM TONIGHT. —TEE.

1. WHAT'S MY FAVORITE FOOD?

Easy. Mallomars cookies.

2. WHAT'S MY IDEA OF A PERFECT DATE?

Flowers, dinner at a cool new restaurant, dancing. Hey, I'm good, aren't I?

3. WHAT BOTHERS ME MORE THAN ANYTHING?

Boredom. Definitely.

4. WHAT'S THE MOST ROMANTIC THING YOU EVER DID FOR ME? (YOU'RE SUPPOSED TO BE MY BOYFRIEND, REMEMBER?)

Uh . . . I think I'll let you decide that one.

5. WHAT KIND OF UNDERWEAR DO I WEAR?

Tee? I really don't want to know the answer to that.

CHAPTER

Colossally Stupid

2

I so *don't belong here,* Andy thought as he sat on the floor of a seemingly endless, airless hallway *way* too early on a Sunday morning. He was squished in between Tia and a faux blonde who had hit the perfume bottle one too many times. The girl's sickeningly sweet floral scent was making Andy's stomach turn over. Combined with the way she was nuzzling into her boyfriend's arms and calling him "pumpkin" every other second, Andy was getting downright nauseous.

He was also beginning to sweat. Andy tugged at the collar of his green, long-sleeved T-shirt. He wiped his hand across his clammy forehead. Scratch that. He *was* sweating.

"*How* did you talk me into this?" he muttered, turning to Tia.

"Excuse me?" Tia's dark brown eyes opened wide. "*We* decided this was going to be fun, remember?"

Andy stared up at the fluorescent lights. "We did, huh? And you call being crammed in between these

16

people in saunalike conditions for an hour fun?"

"Actually I do," Tia responded. "It's totally enter-taining." She nudged in closer to Andy and dropped her voice to a whisper. "Example—check out the couple next to me. My prediction? If they make the show, the wanna-be actress is dumping his sorry butt the minute it's over."

Andy leaned in slightly to see the couple Tia was referring to. The "wanna-be actress" was fixing her makeup in a silver compact and smoothing out her long, dark hair.

"Okay," the girl said in a cool and practiced-sounding voice, without taking her eyes off her little mirror. "What kind of toothpaste do I use?"

Her skinny, confused-looking boyfriend scratched his head. "Um . . . Crest?"

"Ethan!" The girl snapped her compact shut and glared at him. "Tartar-control Colgate! We've been over this! We're never going to win if you can't keep these things straight!"

Andy couldn't help letting out a little snort. He quickly sat back and covered his mouth with his hand before Miss Actress gave *him* a glare.

"See?" Tia prodded. "This *is* fun. So stop being such a downer, all right?"

Andy dropped his hands in his lap. "Okay, what-ever," he responded, playing with the dirty shoelace on his sneakers. Tia was right. Andy knew he should just make the most of this situation. Still, every time he glanced up and looked at another one of these couples, all he could think about was how a psychiatrist would have a field day with this one: "Gay teen tries to assert his heterosexuality by acting on a game show."

Andy glanced down at his watch. They were now nearing the hour-and-a-half point. Letting out a sigh, he shifted his position on the hard floor, but it was useless. His butt was officially asleep. Which was exactly what Andy wanted to be—asleep in bed. So when the overperfumed blonde poked Andy's side *again* while trying to hug her "pumpkin," Andy finally lost it.

"I'm outta here," he told Tia as he stood up.

"You're leaving?" Tia quickly stood as well. She placed her hands on her hips. "No way—you can't go."

Andy wiped the palms of his hands against his jeans. "Sorry, Tee. I really can't be here another minute." He turned to go, but Tia grabbed his arm. *Hard.* Andy whipped back around.

"Andy," Tia said through her teeth. "We've already waited this long. They're going to call us any minute. It'd be stupid to leave now."

"How do you know?" Andy challenged. "There's still, like, a hundred other couples here." He motioned to the long line of people crowded along the linoleum floor. "It could be another three hours for all we know."

"Marsden and Ramirez?" a loud female voice called out from the other end of the hall.

Tia broke out into a smile. "Or it could be *right now*." She squeezed Andy's arm, which she was still clinging to. "How lucky!"

Andy's shoulders slumped. "Yeah. Lucky." *Wonderful.* Andy knew he had no choice now. He had to go through with this, or Tia would never let him hear the end of it. So he didn't even try to protest as Tia turned and pulled him down the hall, past the other game-show hopefuls. They all seemed to be staring up at Andy and Tia, as if to check out the competition, making Andy feel even more uncomfortable.

When Andy and Tia finally reached the end of the hall, the woman who'd called their names was standing in front of a blue door, holding a clipboard and looking mighty stressed.

"We're Marsden and Ramirez," Tia announced, looking so excited, she was practically jumping up and down.

"Fine," the woman said, barely glancing up from her clipboard. She stepped aside and motioned to the door with a tip of her head. "Go on in."

Tia glanced at Andy, her big eyes full of enthusiasm. "Cheer up. I promise this'll be a trip."

19

"Whatever," Andy whispered. "Let's just get it over with."

Shaking her head in obvious frustration, Tia turned back around and pushed open the door. Andy held his breath as they stepped inside. He felt a slight sense of relief when he saw that there were only two people in the stark, high-ceilinged room—a guy and a woman. For some reason, whenever Andy had pictured the "judges," he'd imagined a stern-looking line of middle-aged men in suits. But these people looked like they were in their late twenties, and they were both dressed sort of hip—the curly-haired woman had an eyebrow pierce, and the scruffy-looking guy was sporting a five-o'clock shadow.

"Come on in. Sit down," the woman said, gesturing to the only other two chairs in the room—brown folding ones on the other side of the long, rectangular table where she and the guy were sitting. As Andy and Tia walked over and dropped down into the seats, the woman went on to say, "I'm Mika, and this is Brad."

"Mika," Andy repeated, leaning back in his chair. "Cool name."

Mika pushed a wayward curl away from her face and smiled. "Thanks."

"Good move." Brad gave Andy a nod of approval. "Flattery will get you everywhere with us."

Tia and Andy both smiled, and suddenly Andy felt at ease.

"So," Mika began, looking down at the pink form that Andy and Tia had filled out when they'd first arrived at the studio that morning. "It says here that you've been together for two years."

"Right," Tia responded, pulling down on her silk top. "We started going out sophomore year."

Mika glanced up from the sheet. She looked from Tia to Andy. "That's a long time. You two must really love each other."

Andy tapped his fingers on the table. And then he couldn't help it. He let out a small laugh.

Brad leaned forward on the imitation-wood table and raised an eyebrow. "Something funny?"

Andy shrugged. "No, it's just that, well, we *do* love each other and everything. But it's sort of a love-hate thing, you know?"

"Excuse me?" Tia snapped. Andy didn't even turn to look at Tia. He could feel her shooting him the death glare. But Andy ignored it—he knew where he was going with this one. He was simply giving the judges what they wanted—an entertaining couple.

Mika's mouth drew up into a half smile. "No, we don't know." She placed both hands flat on the table and regarded Andy with blue, wide-open eyes. "Enlighten us."

"Yes, please," Tia added in a tight voice. "Enlighten us."

"Hold up. I didn't mean it how it sounded," Andy backtracked. "What I meant was, yeah, Tee and I love each other. But sometimes it feels like we're together because that's just how it has to be." He fingered a spot on the edge of the table where the dark brown rubber edge was starting to peel off. "Like, it's meant to be.... Basically, I can't imagine life without her."

"Oh, honey, that's so sweet!" Tia reached over and squeezed Andy's hand, smiling. Andy winked back at her.

"Nice save, buddy," Brad commented. He gulped down a sip from a can of soda. "Very impressive."

And that was all the encouragement Andy needed. For the next couple of questions he was *on*, playing the part of Tia's boyfriend so well that at times even *he* wondered if there was a possibility he was straight. In fact, Andy was having so much fun talking with Mika and Brad that he was sorry when Mika said they were done and could move on.

"We're done *already?*" Andy asked, standing up.

"With this part, yes," Mika explained. She reached over and grabbed another couple's form off the stack to the left of her. "But if you go to that green door over there, Matt will show you to the waiting area. And in a little while we'll announce who made the cut for tomorrow's interview."

Andy's face fell. "Another waiting area?" This was fun and all, but he didn't think his butt could handle an extra hour or two on the linoleum floor.

"Don't worry. This one's much nicer than the last," Brad assured him.

"If you say so," Andy responded.

Andy and Tia said their good-byes and crossed the room to the green door. Andy was expecting to find another long hallway when Tia pushed open the door. Instead they were greeted by a *very* cute twenty-something-looking guy with hazel eyes and dark hair, holding a clipboard and wearing a headset.

"Hey, I'm Matt," the guy said, flashing them a toothpaste-commercial grin. "Waiting room's this way."

As Matt walked ahead, Tia tugged on Andy's arm and mouthed the words, "So hot." Andy shook his head in amusement. Leave it to Tia to try to score a boyfriend while auditioning for a couples game show.

But as Matt glanced back at Andy and Tia and gestured for them to walk ahead into a room, Andy did have to agree with Tia. The guy *was* good-looking.

"If you two can sit tight here, we'll let you know what's up in a little while," Matt told them as they stepped inside.

23

Whoa. Andy crossed his lanky arms over his chest and glanced around the souped-up room in surprise. Cozy oversized couches, a big-screen TV, and a little juice-bar area were *not* what he was expecting. "I think I can manage to hang here," he joked.

"Yeah," Tia agreed, looking around as well. "Where's everyone else?" she asked.

"Ah, there's the good news." Matt hugged his clipboard close to his nicely built chest, wiggling his eyebrows. "You guys made the first cut—this is a room full of maybes. Some couples got negged right after their interview and already went on their merry ways."

"Really? Cool." Tia's eyes sparkled.

"Well, chill out and relax," Matt told them. "Help yourself to whatever's in the fridge."

"Thanks." Andy nodded. And as he crossed the room to open the fridge and pull out a can of Coke, he had to agree with Tia. This *was* cool. A lush venue, fun people, and the possibility of a trip to New York?

Andy popped open his soda can. Suddenly he wanted to *win* this thing.

Ken Matthews glanced down at his Ironman watch on Sunday afternoon. It was two-fifteen. He had now officially put off calling Melissa Fox for a complete hour. *Okay. Enough,* he told himself, bouncing his leg up and down as he sat on the edge of his bed. *Just do it.*

In a quick movement Ken reached to pick his cordless phone up off his plaid comforter. But just as swiftly, he placed it down again, letting go of the phone as if it were a hot potato.

Sighing, Ken dropped his head in his hands, rubbing his thick, blond hair. He knew that no one would exactly blame him for not wanting to call Melissa. The girl could be downright nasty when she was angry, and given the way Ken had broken up with her on Friday, angry was probably understating how she felt toward him.

Ken lifted his head, clasping his hands. Still, he knew the right thing to do was to talk to her, to at least explain his actions so that she didn't hate him so much.

Ken stood and walked across his floor to his desk. He lifted one of his football trophies and fidgeted with the shiny brass figurine on its top. The more Ken thought about this whole Melissa-Will mess, the more he realized that those two were the ones who were meant to be together. Ken should never have even figured into the equation. And he knew it was nuts, but Ken felt like he needed to relay this information to

Melissa. He didn't exactly know why it mattered to him whether Will and Melissa ever went out again, except for the fact that he felt partly responsible for their breakup. That was something he wasn't proud of.

Ken swallowed. And there was another thing—if Ken was truly honest with himself. *If I help bring Will and Melissa back together, then maybe—maybe there's a shot that Maria and I can—* Ken shook his head, not even allowing himself to continue with that thought. *Maria has nothing to do with this,* he told himself. *This is just about Melissa.*

Of course, this wouldn't be about *anyone* if Ken didn't pick up the stupid phone and call her already. Letting out a shaky breath, Ken closed his eyes. *You can do this,* he thought. *Melissa might not even be that bad. She might accept your apology.*

Okay. Ken opened his eyes. He was ready. He quickly walked over and scooped up his cordless, dialing Melissa's number before he could chicken out again.

She answered on the second ring. "Hello?"

"Melissa? . . . It's Ken." He gripped the phone tightly, wincing as he spoke.

There was a heavy beat of silence. "Yes?"

Ouch. Her voice couldn't have been icier. Ken dropped down on his bed and gripped the phone more tightly, his free hand forming into a tense fist.

"Look, I just wanted to say I'm sorry about—about the way everything came out on Friday." Drawing in a breath, Ken paused, waiting for Melissa to acknowledge his statement. But he was met with dead silence.

"I, uh, know it was very sudden," Ken continued, tugging at the neckline of his LA Rams T-shirt. "But, well, you must have realized that we weren't really clicking, right? That we just didn't make a good couple?"

There was another long silence, and for a moment Ken wondered if Melissa was even listening. He was about to ask if she was still there when she finally spoke up.

"Is that all?" she asked crisply.

Ken licked his lips. *So much for accepting my apology,* he thought, his stomach twisting. He stood and walked over to his window, fidgeting with the blue blinds. This had been a colossally stupid idea.

Still, Ken realized, he shouldn't hang up yet. If he could just say one more thing to her, plant a seed of an idea in her brain, this conversation might not be totally useless.

"Well, yeah," he responded. "But also . . . listen. I've been thinking about you and Will."

"What?" Melissa snapped. If it was possible, her tone of voice dropped several degrees colder.

27

"Just hold on a second," Ken said. "It's so obvious that you and Will should be together. And after the way he came through at the game the other night, it sort of seems like he's getting himself back in shape. . . . I think maybe you should give him another chance."

"You do?"

Ken froze. Melissa had given him an actual response. Maybe he'd struck a chord with her. "Yeah. I do."

"Well, you know what *I* think?" she asked.

Ken opened his mouth to respond, but Melissa cut him off before he could say a word. "That I don't need your idiotic matchmaking advice. Or your pity. Thank you." And then she clicked off, leaving the dial tone to sound in Ken's ear. *Nice job, Matthews,* Ken thought as he slowly walked over to place the receiver back in its cradle.

Well, that had accomplished a lot. Now she *really* hated him.

I wish I could sleep forever, Melissa thought as she lay deep under her comforter, staring up at the moldings on her ceiling. She was just so *tired*—of everyone and everything. This was her senior year. It was supposed to be perfect. Instead it was perfectly terrible, and everything was falling apart.

And now Ken has the nerve to call me up and try to tell me what to do with my life, she thought, sitting up

28

and pushing her long, dark brown hair away from her face. What did he expect her to do? *Thank* him or something? *He is such a jerk,* she said to herself.

There was a knock on Melissa's door, followed by the sound of her mother's voice. "Melissa? Can I come in?"

Oh, wonderful. Melissa lay all the way back, resting her head against her pillow. More than anything, Melissa wanted to answer no to her mother's question, but she knew it wasn't an option. Her mother would simply walk right in anyway.

"Yes," Melissa called, digging herself deeper under the soft blanket.

Mrs. Fox's mouth dropped open the minute she stepped inside. "Melissa! It's four o'clock!" she said, placing her hands on her slender hips. "*What* are you doing?"

"Resting," Melissa responded quietly, rolling onto her side.

Mrs. Fox marched over and perched herself on the edge of Melissa's bed. Then she went ahead and pulled down the covers, exposing Melissa in her T-shirt and sweats.

"*Mom,*" Melissa protested, annoyed. Sitting up, she let out an exaggerated sigh. This was precisely why Melissa didn't want her to come inside in the first place.

Mrs. Fox's eyebrows furrowed together, causing worry lines to form across her pale forehead. "You can't lie in bed all day. I thought you were going to get started with your college applications this weekend."

Melissa suppressed a moan. Not *this* conversation again. Her life was in ruins all around her, and she was supposed to care about applications? "I'm not in the mood," she stated flatly.

"Melissa, this is not acceptable." Mrs. Fox shook her head, reaching over to pick a piece of lint out of her daughter's hair. "I'm sorry that things haven't worked out with Ken, but you can't let it affect your future. You have to move on."

Melissa stared back at her mother and held on tightly to the edge of her comforter, anger and frustration starting to rise up inside her. What did *she* know about what Melissa was going through? What did she know about breakups and humiliation? Melissa's mother met her father when she was *fourteen,* at which point he fell in love with her, continued to worship the ground she walked on, and promptly married her at the age of twenty. And now she was telling Melissa to "move on."

"I really don't want to talk about this right now," Melissa said tightly, sliding out of her bed. She walked over to her oak dresser and pulled her SVH cheerleading sweatshirt out of the bottom drawer, putting it on over her slender frame.

"You *never* want to talk about this," Mrs. Fox argued, standing as well. "Have you even decided exactly where you're applying yet?"

Melissa sat down on her desk chair, hugging her knees to her chest as her head began to pound. She did *not* want to have this conversation. Anytime she tried to think about where she was applying, she was reminded of the fact that she was supposed to go to Michigan with Will. *That* had been the plan. And even after Will's accident, she'd still been headed for Michigan—only with Ken instead. But now she had no one and nowhere to go. No future at all.

She sighed. "Not exactly. Can we talk about this tomorrow?"

A rush of color tinged Mrs. Fox's cheeks. "No, we cannot! Your deadlines are looming, you still have to visit some schools, not to mention your essays, and—"

"Mom!" Melissa broke in, her voice louder than she'd expected. "*Please! Get off my case!*"

Her mother's light eyes flashed, her mouth forming into a straight line. "Melissa Fox. Do *not* speak that way to me."

"Can you just leave me alone?" Melissa pleaded, a tightness forming in her throat.

"Well, clearly you're incapable of logical conversation

31

right now, so yes, I will leave you alone," Mrs. Fox told her shortly. "But we *will* finish this discussion. And you better have some answers." She gave her daughter one final penetrating stare, then turned and stalked out.

Once her door was closed, Melissa dropped her head in her hands, trying to keep from crying. Why was everyone so aggravating lately? She sniffled, rubbing her nose with the cuff of her sweatshirt. It was as if no one understood her. She felt totally alone. There wasn't one person she could talk to.

Except Will. Melissa knew that just the sound of his voice would calm her down. She reached and pulled a tissue out of the box on her desk, blowing her nose. He always knew exactly what to say. At least, he used to.

Melissa paused for a moment, thinking about what Ken had said to her. Could Will want her back? Should she call him?

But then, just as quickly as the thought entered her brain, it left. *Don't be stupid,* Melissa told herself, crumpling up the tissue. *Ken was only right about one thing—that he and I don't belong together.*

Wiping a tear from her cheek, Melissa tossed the wadded-up tissue in the trash can under her desk.

But Ken doesn't know the first thing about Will.

Elizabeth Wakefield

<u>Possible</u> <u>reactions</u> <u>I</u> <u>might</u> <u>have</u>
<u>when</u> <u>I</u> <u>see</u> <u>Conner</u> <u>for</u> <u>the</u> <u>first</u> <u>time:</u>

I'll cry.
I'll run in the other direction.
I'll throw up.
I won't be able to speak.
I'll do a combination of all of the
above.

CHAPTER  3

Home. Finally.

"We are so going to make the cut," Tia told Andy as she munched on some pretzels. They were sitting side by side on a green velvet couch in the Alcon Studios waiting room. In the hour that they'd been hanging out there, only four more couples had come in. Tia took this to be a highly positive sign.

Andy leaned back into the couch. "Don't say that. You might jinx us."

"Not possible." Tia threw her short legs up on the low black coffee table, crossing one over the other. "We're too lucky. And we totally rocked that interview."

Andy let out an exaggerated, self-satisfied sigh. "Yes, well, I *did* do a good job in there."

"Not just good." Tia shook her head, then pulled the scrunchie off her wrist and wrapped it around her long, wavy hair. "*Great.* You know, for all your moaning and groaning, you really came through."

Andy shrugged. "What can I say? I aim to please."

Tia let out a snort. "Excuse me if I have a hard time buying *that* one," she commented.

"You guys hanging in all right?"

Tia glanced up to see Matt, the cute crew guy, standing before her. *No, make that extremely* hot *crew guy,* she amended, her heart fluttering in her rib cage. Those hazel eyes, that thick, dark hair, that olive skin—not to mention that *body* that was so clearly buffed underneath his worn-in, gray-green T-shirt. This guy was totally Tia's type. Wait a minute—what was she thinking? He was *everyone's* type.

Tia sat up, dropping her feet to the floor and quickly pulling the scrunchie out of her hair to let the thick strands cascade down her shoulders. "Are you kidding?" she said to Matt, flashing him a smile. "We've got food, drinks, TV, plus all the people watching you could ask for." Tia motioned around the room, signaling to the various couples that were camped out on couches, love seats, tall stools by the bar area, and the light gray carpeting in front of the television. "We are *plenty* entertained."

"Glad to hear it." Matt dropped down onto the wide armrest next to Tia and rested his clipboard against his knee. "These auditions can be kinda tedious."

As Tia looked back at Matt, all she could think was that talking with him wasn't even close to being tedious.

Tia shrugged and widened her eyes. "If we win,

it'll be worth it." She leaned forward, lightly placing her hand on Matt's well-toned arm. "Do you have any say in this? You *will* vote for us, right?"

Matt let out a laugh. "I'm just a lowly PA—a production assistant. But I'll be sure to put in a good word." He stood, sticking a hand in his back jeans pocket. "Gotta go check on the other couples. I'll be back in a few."

"Can't wait," Tia responded, still smiling. She stared after him as he strolled toward a couple by the bar. Then she turned to Andy. "He's coming back!"

Andy rolled his eyes. "Don't you think you were laying it on just a wee bit thick?"

"Who, me?" Tia joked, scooping up another handful of pretzels from the bowl in front of her. So Andy had picked up on her flirting—big deal. What was she going to do? Not flirt with the guy? *Please.* "Come on, you have to admit the guy is gorgeous. Besides, there's nothing wrong with a little flirtation."

"Um, yeah, there is," Andy argued. "Especially if you're auditioning for a *couples* game show and you're supposed to be my girlfriend. Looks a little suspect if you're hitting on the staff, Tee."

Tia bit her lip. *Oops.* Andy did have a point there. "Oh, right," she said, crossing her arms over her chest and sinking farther into the couch. "I see what you mean."

"Okay, then," Andy replied. He ran a hand through his red hair. "So chill on the eye-batting routine, all right?"

Tia glanced down and kicked at the carpeting. "Fine," she said with a sigh. Just her luck. She'd met the first guy she was truly into in a long time, and he was off-limits.

And he's coming back already, Tia noticed, her hopes lifting as she spotted Matt crossing the room, heading straight for her and Andy.

"Missed us, huh?" she called as he approached, tossing her hair behind her shoulder. Andy gave her a quick nudge, but Tia ignored it. She couldn't help herself. It was physically impossible for her not to flirt with the guy. Andy would just have to deal.

"I needed a return to normalcy," Matt explained, this time sitting down on the coffee table in front of Tia and Andy. He lowered his voice, leaning in a bit. "Some of these couples take this thing a little too seriously. They can be sort of intense to be around."

Tia beamed back at him. Clearly he preferred their company to anyone else's. This was a good thing. A *very* good thing.

Andy laughed. "We've already witnessed that for ourselves."

Matt glanced from Andy to Tia, scratching his chiseled chin. "You know, come to think of it, you guys are one of the most mellow couples I've witnessed. Usually people are all nervous and quizzing each other to prepare for tomorrow, just in case they make the cut."

"Yeah, well, we just know each other *so well*," Andy said, slinging an arm around Tia's shoulders. "We've been together a long time."

"That's cool." Matt nodded, clasping his hands. "Hope you guys make it."

Tia's neck muscles tightened at Andy's touch. He was totally ruining her chances with Matt! She was certain that if Matt knew she was single, he'd hit on her. He was already being all flirty with her as it was, flashing her killer smiles and looking at her *that way,* with an amused glint in his hazel eyes. Part of her wanted to throw in the towel and tell Matt the truth. After all, her love life was more important than a stupid game show, wasn't it?

Then something Matt said suddenly registered with her. *Hope you guys make it.* Tia sat up straight, forcing Andy to remove his arm from her shoulders and pointedly ignoring the look of annoyance that Andy gave her. For the first time since this whole audition process had begun, Tia found herself half hoping that they *wouldn't* get called back. Then she'd be free and clear to ask Matt out.

Just then Mika, the woman who'd interviewed them earlier, stepped inside the doorway. The room fell silent at the sight of her. Someone switched off the TV.

"Well," Mika said, seemingly a bit taken aback that all eyes were trained on her, "I'll just go ahead and call the names of those who made it since that's all you guys want to hear anyway." She lifted the piece of paper that was in her hand and began to read. "Okay. Chesler and Flax . . ."

"Yes!" A tall blonde jumped up off a love seat and kissed her stocky boyfriend.

Tia shot a glance at Matt, who had turned around to listen to Mika. She grasped the edge of the soft couch, chewing the inside of her lip. What did she want to happen? On the one hand, it would be cool to be on the game show. But on the other, it would be more than cool to go out with Matt.

"Valentine and Hudson . . ."

"Woo-hoo!" A guy with a shaved head pumped his fist as his petite girlfriend squealed with excitement. The guy then picked her up and twirled her in the air.

Then again, Tia thought as she took in this happy-winner scene, *the whole reason I came on this show was because I had no social life. Going out with Matt would definitely change* that.

Suddenly Tia knew what she wanted. She closed her eyes, gripping the couch cushion more tightly.

"Marsden and Ramirez . . ."

Tia's eyes flew open just as Andy held out a hand to slap her five. "All right!" he said, laughing. "We made it."

Matt turned back around and smiled at both of them. "Congrats, guys."

Tia's stomach sank as she looked into Matt's gorgeous eyes. She forced a smile, then halfheartedly slapped Andy back.

"Yeah," she said flatly. "Great . . .we made it."

Conner tried to ignore the knots that were beginning to form in his stomach as the bus he'd boarded in Callas neared Sweet Valley. But each time he spotted another highway landmark out of his grime-covered window—the mall, then Lucky Burger, then Ed's Hardware Emporium—Conner felt his abdomen muscles twist even more tightly, and he couldn't deny it—he was freaked about coming home.

Rubbing his clammy palms against his soft, worn-in jeans, Conner took his eyes off the window. He figured that not staring out at all of his childhood hangouts might help him to calm down. Still, when he glanced to his right and looked at his neighbor—a gray-haired man with a scruffy beard and pockmarks who reeked of stale cigarette smoke—Conner decided that his best option would be to stare straight ahead.

This turned out to be a good decision because as Conner inhaled the nonventilated, stagnant air, all the while hearing the boisterous woman behind him's commentary on the rising price of raisin bran, Conner suddenly just wanted to get off this bus. *Fast.*

He turned out to be lucky because at that moment the driver made a quick right, then brought the bus to a stop, the brakes screeching.

"All out for Sweet Valley," the driver announced, pulling the lever to swing open the bus door.

Thank God. Conner threw his head back against the seat and closed his eyes. *Okay,* he told himself. *You're fine. You'll just hop in a cab, go home, and you'll be fine.* He opened his eyes and stood, climbing over the guy next to him since the old man seemed to find it too much trouble to move and give Conner some room to pass.

As Conner pulled his duffel bag down from the overhead bin and made his way up the aisle, the nerves in his stomach began to fire off again. And he was hit with an unpleasant realization—this wasn't going to be easy. Not by a long shot. In fact, this whole coming-home experience could downright suck.

But when Conner stepped out of the bus and felt the crisp, cool evening air hit his face, his nerves settled a little. He shouldered his bag and was heading straight for an empty taxicab that was idling at the

41

curb when he saw his mom and his sister, Megan, hurrying toward him.

Whoa, he thought, dropping his duffel down on the concrete sidewalk, his heart rate picking up a bit. He wasn't expecting *this.* He'd told his mother yesterday that he'd make it home on his own.

"Conner!" Megan exclaimed as soon as she reached him. She quickly pulled him into a tight hug. "It's so good to see you."

Conner hugged her back, feeling his muscles relax. He even smiled slightly as he tightened his grip around her. She smelled like Dove soap and that fruity shampoo she'd been using for years. Conner pulled back and kissed her soft forehead. Basically, she smelled like home.

"Good to see you too, Sandy," he said, using his nickname for her.

"Honey." Conner's mother placed a light hand on his shoulder, and he turned to look at her. "I hope it's okay that we came," she said, pushing a wisp of her permed blond hair away from her eyes. "We just couldn't let you take a cab home."

Conner glanced down at his work boots, shifting his weight from one foot to the other. "Yeah," he told her. "It's fine." As he said the words, he realized they were true. He even felt kind of glad to see his mom and Megan.

42

"Conner," Mrs. Sandborn said, her eyes clouding with obvious emotion. "We missed you."

As she reached out and gave him a hug, Conner wondered if things would finally start to change between them. It wasn't like he'd totally forgotten just how far from perfect his mom was. But at least Conner could now understand firsthand what she had gone through.

Mrs. Sandborn lifted her head from his shoulder and gave him a kiss on the cheek. Then she pulled back and smoothed out the hem of her black sweater. "C'mon," she said, tipping her head in the direction of the parking lot behind them. "Let's go home."

Ten minutes later Conner found himself in the passenger seat of his mother's Mercedes. They were seconds away from their house, and he was feeling much more relaxed. He hadn't spoken much the whole ride—he'd basically just listened to Megan catch him up on what had been going on with her life—but he was surprised at what a calming effect being around his family was having on him. And he'd actually been dreading this encounter.

Maybe it'll be the same deal with other people, Conner thought as his mother made the left onto their block. *People like Liz.* Conner swallowed, fidgeting with the door lock as those nervous vibes swam across his stomach again.

43

Yeah, right. He took in the sight of his house as his mom pulled up the driveway. *Seeing Liz is going to be* nothing *like this.*

Whatever. Odds are slim she even wants to talk to me, he thought. Conner got out and walked around to the trunk to lift up his bag. He glanced over at his cherished Mustang.

"You better not have missed that car more than you missed me," Megan teased, stepping up beside him, her green eyes bright and playful.

Conner reached over and tousled her long, red hair. "I don't know. It's a close call."

Megan rolled her eyes, then headed toward the house with Conner following her. "Figured as much," she said, opening the front door.

They stepped inside, and Conner saw that nothing about his house had changed. Same wood floors, same deep red oriental carpet, same off-white walls. And that was fine with Conner. He'd had enough change for a long time.

"I didn't make a big dinner or anything," his mom said. "I figured you might just want some time to unpack and unwind on your own. But there's plenty of food if you're hungry."

Conner rubbed his eyes, feeling a sense of relief wash over him. As much as he'd surprisingly enjoyed his time with his family so far, there was only so much he could take. His mom was right—he needed his alone time.

"No," Conner responded, walking toward the stairs. "I'm just gonna go up to my room for now."

Mrs. Sandborn nodded, her eyes filled with understanding. "All right. Fine."

Conner headed up the stairs, down the long hallway, and into his narrow room. With his iron-frame bed by the wall and his guitar propped up in the corner, his bedroom looked just like it had when he left. Conner dropped his bag down on the floor and sat on his mattress, glancing around and letting out a heavy breath.

He was here. Home. Finally.

Conner's eyes fell on the black phone that sat on the wooden night table next to his bed. Now that he was by himself in his room, he could finally do the one thing he'd been thinking about ever since he'd boarded that bus tonight.

He could call Elizabeth.

Conner picked up the receiver and stared at it. *Right,* he thought sarcastically. *I'm sure she'll be so happy to hear from me.* Then again, it was Elizabeth. She was capable of supreme acts of forgiveness. Conner continued to stare at the phone. *You've tested her on* that *plenty of times.*

Shaking his head, Conner finally did dial a girl's number. And she picked up on the first ring.

"Tee," Conner said, tugging at the neckline of his T-shirt. "It's me."

Elizabeth tossed and turned under her sheets, wanting more than anything to just fall asleep. But at the moment that seemed rather impossible. She sighed, kicking the cotton sheets away from her body. Ever since she'd come to the realization that Conner would be home any day now, that one subject had occupied all of her brain space.

Elizabeth sat up and leaned against her headboard, staring blankly across her darkened room. Of course, the topic presented itself in many different variations. For the last thirty-six hours a cycle of questions had repeatedly circled through her mind—*Will Conner be different when he gets back? Will he want to see me? Will I want to see him? What will I say? What will he say?* . . .

Enough! Elizabeth slid out of bed and marched across the room to her desk. She had spent enough time—no, make that *far too much* time—thinking and worrying about Conner this year. She sat down at her desk chair and turned on her computer, figuring that she could at least funnel this wired energy toward finishing her story for creative writing.

But there was one thing that made Elizabeth especially angry with herself, she realized as she waited

46

for her computer to boot up. It was the fact that even now, even after all she'd been through with Conner, she knew deep in her heart that she still cared about him. A lot. Why else would she be spending all this time thinking about him?

Then again, maybe it's the not knowing, Elizabeth realized. She brought her feet up onto her chair. Maybe what was really bothering her was that she didn't know the exact day Conner would be returning. And it was her fear of being caught off guard, of not being prepared, that was really freaking her out.

That's totally possible, Elizabeth thought, relaxing back into her chair. She dropped her feet back down on the carpet, her brain defogging somewhat. She grabbed the mouse and clicked open the file she'd been working on. Now she might even get some work done.

The phone rang, and Elizabeth immediately grabbed it off her desk, not wanting it to wake up her parents. "Hello?"

"Hi, it's Tia. Hope it's not too late."

Elizabeth swiveled her chair around. "It's okay. What's going on?"

"Um . . . not much," Tia said, a serious *but* dangling off the end of her response.

Elizabeth chewed on a nail while she waited for Tia to continue, but nothing else came out. "So you just called to chat?" she asked.

"Not exactly," Tia admitted. "I wasn't sure if I should call to tell you this, but—" She paused. "Okay. Here it is—Conner called me. He's home. And he'll be at school tomorrow."

Elizabeth blinked. She bit her lip, not realizing that several seconds had passed without her responding.

"Liz? You okay?"

"What? Oh, yeah, yes. I'm fine," she said, standing up and grabbing at the edge of her loose-fitting pink T-shirt, suddenly needing to do something— anything—with her hands. "It just took me a minute to—"

"I'm sorry," Tia broke in. "I shouldn't have called. I didn't mean to get you upset. I just wanted you to be prepared."

"No, I know," Elizabeth said. She held a hand to her chest and closed her eyes, trying to calm herself down. "It's fine. *I'm* fine. Really. Thanks."

"Yeah?" Tia asked, sounding unsure.

No. Not at all.

Elizabeth opened her eyes and walked over to her window, sitting down on the cushioned ledge. "Yes," she lied. "Don't worry about it."

"All right," Tia conceded. "You know, Liz, he sounded okay . . . better."

Elizabeth hugged her knees to her chest as a

48

lump started to rise in her throat. Her pulse was sounding in her ears, and she knew only one thing for sure. She had to get off the phone. *Now.*

"Okay. Good. Well, thanks for calling, Tee." Elizabeth stood again and ran a hand through her tangled blond hair. "But I gotta go. See you tomorrow?"

"Yeah . . . okay," Tia responded. "Sure."

Elizabeth was about to say good-bye when Tia quickly added, "Wait. You *sure* you're okay?"

"Yes," Elizabeth said quickly, feeling her cheeks flush with emotion. "I promise."

"All right," Tia replied, not sounding at all convinced. "But call me later if you want to talk. I'll be up."

"Thanks. Good night," Elizabeth said, then immediately clicked off the phone. She couldn't have managed to listen to Tia for one more second. She needed a moment to process this information—to accept the fact that she was actually going to see Conner tomorrow.

Elizabeth sat down at the foot of her bed and tried to let it all sink in. *Conner's back. He'll be at school. Tomorrow.* Her stomach twisted. Tomorrow.

There went her not-knowing theory. Because now she knew for sure that Conner was home. And she was still completely freaked out—if not more so.

Letting out a frustrated sigh, Elizabeth reached over and flicked on her dome-shaped overhead fixture. *Might as well have some light,* she figured.

After all, there was no way she was getting any sleep tonight.

Alanna Feldman

<u>Things</u> to <u>do</u> when <u>I</u> get <u>home</u> from rehab:

1. Call Conner.
2. Visit Grandma.
3. Meet with my teachers to catch up with work.
4. Apologize to Sarah.
5. Call Conner.
6. Find a new after-school job.
7. Call Conner.

CHAPTER 4
Mysterious Ways

A new week, Ken thought as he pulled his Trooper in between a white Cabriolet and a rusty old Dodge in Sweet Valley High's crowded parking lot on Monday morning. *This one's gotta be better than the last.* He switched off the radio and cut the engine, then grabbed his blue backpack off the passenger seat.

Whatever. At least it's a fresh start, Ken thought as he stepped out of his car, slamming the door behind him. Shouldering his backpack and locking up his SUV, he glanced around, taking in the hordes of students who were streaming toward the school's sprawling, low buildings. He then took a moment to squint up at the bright blue, cloudless sky, the strong rays of sunshine warming his cheeks. Good weather was always helpful in kicking the week off right— maybe this was an omen. Maybe this was the week that everything was going to change for him. Feeling recharged, Ken pulled down on his navy blue polo shirt and started to head toward the school entrance.

After dodging a skinny guy on a bike who nearly ran right into him, Ken spotted Melissa off to his left, getting out of her car. For a split second he felt uneasy at the sight of her, but then it suddenly struck him as another omen. Maybe, just maybe, now that she'd had some time to think about their conversation, to let Ken's words sink in, maybe Melissa would accept Ken's apology. That would *really* get this week rolling in a positive spin.

Ken stopped in place for a moment, watching Melissa as she pulled her leather backpack out of the backseat and flipped her long, brown hair behind her shoulder. *She doesn't* look *angry,* he thought, shifting his weight from one foot to the other. *But she doesn't exactly look happy either.* Then again, Melissa never looked all that happy—even when she was. A serious intensity in her large, light blue eyes with her mouth formed into an unemotional straight line was basically Melissa's default expression. *Might as well test the waters,* Ken reasoned. Besides, it was 8 A.M. How mean could she be so early in the morning?

Melissa was starting to walk away from her car, so Ken jogged over to catch up with her. "Melissa," he called out.

She stopped moving and glanced over her shoulder. When she saw Ken, her eyes glazed over. She

53

crossed her slender arms over her chest. "What?" she asked, giving him a withering stare.

Oo-kay. Yeah. This is a bad mood, all right, Ken thought as he stumbled over to her, now regretting this move altogether. He cleared his throat. "Um, nothing," he said lamely, rubbing his hands together. "Just . . . hi."

Melissa simply stared at him for a second longer, her thin lips forming into a slight scowl. Then she rolled her eyes and stalked off.

Ken stood there frozen for a moment, dumbstruck as he watched Melissa quickly walk up the steps toward the entrance's open double doors. He had the answer to one question, he realized, running a hand through his wavy blond hair. *Very* mean. Melissa could be very mean first thing in the morning.

But it's also just a front, he thought, slowly walking toward the school steps himself. By this point Ken knew Melissa pretty well, and he had somewhat of a handle on her mysterious ways (as much as anyone could have, at least). He was certain that there was a whole load of emotions just waiting to break through Melissa's glacierlike surface.

Ken headed up the steps, weaving his way around two sophomore girls who were sitting in his path, one of the girls giggling and blushing as he passed. The problem was, Ken was *not* going to be the one to chip away at her surface. That was for sure.

In fact, there was probably only one person who'd be able to break through to Melissa. And as Ken walked through the school, he decided that he'd approach that person next.

Yeah, it was probably stupid. Still, it couldn't be as disastrous as Ken's encounter with Melissa had been. Right?

Elizabeth rubbed her red-rimmed eyes as she stumbled out of homeroom that morning. It wasn't even 9 A.M., and already she didn't know how she was going to make it through the day. Letting out a yawn, Elizabeth turned left down the hall, heading for her locker. She'd gotten a grand total of three hours of sleep last night, and now she felt like she was sleep walking. When she added the fact that she was still beyond anxious about seeing Conner onto her sleep-deprived state, she wished more than anything that she could just play sick and go home.

But you really can't, Elizabeth reminded herself, wrapping her cotton cardigan more closely around her body. Not only would she get way behind in her classes if she cut out today, but she also had a mandatory *Oracle* meeting after school. With the amount of work she had to complete for the school newspaper, odds were she'd be in the *Oracle* office until at least five.

At which point I'll just collapse, she thought, moving over to grab a sip from the water fountain. *If I don't break down before then.* Elizabeth stepped away from the metal fountain, trying to figure out if there was any possible way to put off her *Oracle* meeting until tomorrow. She was so distracted that she didn't even see anyone coming until she'd walked right into someone's purple T-shirted chest.

"Sorry," she said, moving back. When she glanced up, she found herself looking right into Evan's eyes. "Oh . . . sorry," she repeated, her cheeks flushing. "I didn't see you."

Evan raised his dark eyebrows. "Yeah. I could tell. You a bit out of it today?"

Elizabeth glanced down at the floor. *Great.* Apparently her sister wasn't the only one who could read her expressions. *So what will Conner think when he sees me looking like this? Will he know how freaked out I am to see him?*

Elizabeth forced the Conner thoughts out of her brain and looked back up at Evan. "You could say that." She paused, pushing a strand of hair behind her ear. "So. Have a good weekend?"

"Yeah, I did." Evan hooked a finger through one of his beat-up corduroy pants' belt loops and paused, watching Elizabeth carefully, his brown eyes searching. "I, you know, hung out with Jade on Friday night."

Elizabeth forced a smile. As much as she was slightly weirded out to think that Evan and Jade were seeing each other, she wanted to make it clear that she was perfectly okay with it. Evan deserved to be happy. "Yes. I know," she said. "Jade seems to be having fun."

Evan grinned. "Yeah, me too." He placed a hand on Elizabeth's shoulder, guiding her over to the side so that a freshman who was holding a precarious-looking science project on a tray could safely pass. After the guy walked by, Evan cleared his throat, pushing some of his long, black hair away from his face. "So. Have you heard that Conner's coming back today?"

Elizabeth's stomach dropped to the floor. As she gripped the straps of her backpack, she told herself she was really going to have to get it together. *If you lose it every time someone mentions his name, what are you going to do when you see him?* she wondered.

"Yes," she said to Evan. "I heard."

"Might be kinda strange at first, huh?" Evan said, his voice softening.

Elizabeth locked eyes with his, grateful that he seemed to understand—as always. She nodded. "Yes."

Evan sighed. He slipped his backpack off his shoulders and lowered it to the floor. "Look. I hate to ask you this, but I was wondering . . ." He paused, scratching his chin. "Are you going to tell him about us?"

Elizabeth blinked. Somehow it still felt weird to think that she and Evan had been an "us," even for such a short time. And she hadn't gotten past imagining the first-meeting stage with Conner to decide whether she should tell him about Evan.

Until now. Elizabeth bit her lip, weighing this out in her brain. Although the concept was still difficult to wrap her mind around, she realized that if she and Conner resumed any sort of relationship—friendship or otherwise—she couldn't keep any secrets from him.

"I guess so," Elizabeth said finally. She crossed her arms over her chest, scrunching her eyebrows together. "Would you be okay with that?"

Evan shrugged and dropped both hands into his baggy front pockets. "I'm not psyched for him to find out, but whatever. Conner deserves to know the truth."

Feeling another chill, Elizabeth hugged herself. "I think so too," she said softly. Her eyes clouding, she gazed off into the middle distance for a moment, trying to imagine what Conner's reaction would be when he found out that his ex-girlfriend and his close friend had had a little fling. But that just gave her another chill.

"Liz?" Evan said.

"Yes. Sorry. I'm here." She placed a hand on Evan's arm. "Would you mind if I was the one to tell Conner? I just think that—"

"Liz," Evan broke in, holding up a hand. "You don't need to explain. It's fine. You can tell him."

Elizabeth smiled slightly in relief. He was such an amazing guy—ridiculously nice.

"Thanks," she said, reaching out to give him a quick hug.

"No problem," Evan responded, hugging her back.

But Elizabeth barely processed his words. She was too busy noticing the fact that Conner had just rounded the corner to come down the hall.

Elizabeth quickly pulled away from Evan as her heart rate raced to warp speed. "See you later," she said. "I've gotta go."

Without waiting for a response, Elizabeth turned around and hurried up the hall, ignoring the fact that Evan was most likely wondering what was wrong with her *and* the fact that she was now walking in the opposite direction from her locker.

Elizabeth knew in that second that she was absolutely not ready to face Conner, nor was she ready for him to see her hugging Evan. She needed an escape—*now*.

Evan slowly picked his backpack up off the floor as he watched Elizabeth hurry down the hall. Scratching his forehead, he did a fast mental replay of their conversation, trying to figure out what had upset Elizabeth. But he came up blank. Still, something had to have sent her rushing off like that, he thought as he turned around to head for class.

And then Evan found himself looking right at Elizabeth's "something." *Conner* was heading in his direction. *Liz must've seen him and flipped,* Evan thought, quickly walking over to his friend. Especially since he had been the rather awkward topic of their conversation. Evan, though, was glad to see the guy—despite everything that had gone down. He'd really missed him.

"McD!" Evan called out as his and Conner's eyes met. "What's going on?"

Conner shook his head and gave Evan a genuine smile, his green eyes bright. It *was* a trademark Conner grin—small and lopsided—but it was real, Evan could tell that much. The guy looked good. Healthy.

"Not a lot," Conner responded. He coughed. "Just back at school."

"Yeah? Well, it's great to see you, man," Evan told Conner. And he meant it. Sure, Conner had been a total pain in the butt right before he left, but Evan hoped that rehab had worked and he was now looking at the old Conner—the one who had been one of his best friends.

"Yeah. You too," Conner said, his tone serious and sincere.

Yep, Evan thought, grinning back at his friend. *He's back. Old Conner's back.*

Conner motioned toward the end of the hall with a nudge of his chin. "Going to math?" he asked, referring to the first-period class they had together.

Evan nodded. "Unfortunately," he responded. But he hesitated before heading for the classroom, wondering if he should ask Conner about what he had gone through at all. *He might need to talk,* Evan reasoned, fidgeting with the black plastic buckle that dangled off his backpack's strap.

"So," Evan began as he and Conner both turned and started to walk. "How did it go? Rehab, I mean."

Conner was silent for a moment. "Fine," he finally responded, though barely audibly.

Evan raised his eyebrows as Conner chose to walk around the other side of an arguing couple. *All right, then,* Evan thought. *Guess he doesn't want to talk.* He was a little worried that Conner would now

61

be annoyed with him, but Conner appeared unfazed as they met on the other side of the couple, his body relaxed and slouching.

"So how's Liz?" Conner asked. Looking ahead instead of at Evan, he scratched the back of his neck. "Saw you with her just now," he went on. "You been hanging out?"

Evan's whole body suddenly tensed up. *Does Conner know?* he wondered, staring down at his brown hiking boots. He glanced back up at Conner. *What the hell do I tell him? "Yeah, sorry, man. I fooled around with her while you were gone. Hope you don't mind"?*

But then Conner looked at Evan in anticipation of a response, and Evan could see that there wasn't a trace of suspicion in his friend's expression. Clearly he just wanted to know how Elizabeth was. And he probably thought that she and Evan were just friends. Which was the truth. Evan swallowed. Now, at least.

"Um, yeah, she's been doing okay," Evan responded as they approached the door to their math classroom. They stepped off to the left by a row of mayonnaise-colored lockers as their classmates streamed inside. "I mean, she was kind of a mess when you first left," he explained. Conner glanced down at his work boots and kicked at the ground.

"But she's really pulled herself together," Evan assured him. "Seriously."

Conner nodded. He lifted his head, looking like he was about to say something more, when the bell to signal the beginning of first period rang. Evan took a step to head for the door when Conner said something. Something that sounded like: "Thanks." His eyes wide, Evan stopped in place.

Conner ran a hand through his scruffy hair. "For telling me I was messed up," he went on. "For making me go." And then, before Evan even had a chance to respond, Conner turned and pushed open the classroom's door, walking inside.

Evan blinked as he watched the door swing closed. That had been one of the most sincere things Conner had ever said to him. Technically, Evan should have been happy about that. His stomach turned over as he slumped his way over to the door. But considering that Conner had just thanked him for being a great friend when Evan had basically gone after Elizabeth behind his back, there was only one reaction Evan was capable of having—technical or otherwise.

The one where he felt like crap.

Evan Plummer

Ways that I've been a good friend to Conner:

- I'm there for him.
- We have fun hanging out.
- I'm a fan of his music.
- I've saved his butt plenty of times.

Ways that I've been a bad friend:
- I went after Elizabeth.

Well . . . somehow that one thing in the bad-friend list seems to cancel all the good-friend things out, doesn't it?

CHAPTER

No Escape 5

Will let out a sigh as the bell rang on Monday afternoon, signaling the end of his last class. Mr. Sullivan, his wiry-haired chemistry teacher, dismissed the students, and Will reached out for his crutches. Leaning on the wooden supports, he slid off his tall metal stool, then performed a balancing act as he grabbed his gray V-necked sweater off his seat and swiped up his backpack from the floor.

Sure, Will was glad that this day was over. But this only marked another afternoon that he would *not* be going to football practice. *Just like every afternoon for the rest of my life,* Will thought miserably.

He headed out into the packed hallway, wondering what he should do with the endless hours of the day laid out before him. *I could overload on fast food,* he thought, making a left toward his locker. Or, even more exciting, he could go home and watch talk show after talk show. The possibilities were truly endless.

"Hey . . . Simmons."

Will stopped moving. He glanced over his right shoulder to see Ken Matthews approaching him. *Or I could stand here and talk to the guy who's become everything I used to be,* Will thought. He grasped the wooden bars on his crutches, his shoulders stiffening.

Ken licked his lips. "Look," he said. "Can we talk for a sec? There's some stuff I want to tell you."

This should be good. "Sure. Whatever."

"Okay. Cool." Ken motioned for Will to follow him into an empty classroom. Even after their sort-of truce at the game Friday night, Will didn't feel like hanging out with the guy. Still, he *was* curious about what Ken had to say.

Will sat down in a chair, resting his crutches on the little desk that was attached to it. He looked at Ken, who stood in front of him. "Okay," Will said. "What?"

"Um, there's a couple of things." Ken cracked his knuckles, then dropped his hands by his sides. "Okay. I'm just gonna say it. Melissa and I broke up the other day . . . and I can tell you're the guy she really wants. She's just way too proud to ever admit it." Ken paused for a moment, as if he was waiting for a response from Will.

But Will simply looked down at the brown desk, his stomach tightening. *Yeah, right,* he thought.

Dumping me to go out with you is a great way to show me that.

Ken let out a deep breath. "Listen, Simmons, I'm sorry—for everything."

Surprised at the statement, Will glanced back up at him.

"It must've looked like I was trying to steal your life from you or something. I wasn't—I swear." Ken fidgeted with his hands. "But I never should've hooked up with Melissa. I know that now."

Will's eyes widened. He tried to find his voice, tried to say *something* in response, but he came up empty.

"You should know that Melissa belongs with you," Ken added quietly.

"Matthews, Melissa and I are never going to happen," Will said quickly. "We're over forever. . . . But I was way off about you."

Ken raised his eyebrows. A wave of relief seemed to wash over his features. "Good," Ken said. "I mean, I'm glad you think so."

Taking in Ken's earnest expression, Will suddenly felt like the lowest form of scum on the planet. *The guy gets manipulated by Melissa, and you take it out on him?* Will thought, guilt creeping over him. *You arrange to get him freakin' injured?*

"Ken, there's something I gotta tell *you*," Will

67

said, the words flowing out before he could even stop them.

Ken leaned against the back of the chair in front of Will's. "Okay. Sure."

Man. Will drew in a sharp breath. How was he going to explain *this?* "Last Friday. At the game." The nerves in Will's stomach were now having a full-out party, and the back of his neck began to dampen with sweat. "I actually did want something—something terrible—to happen to you." His mouth drying up, Will couldn't look Ken in the eyes. He stared down at his hands. "But then when something *did* happen, I felt horrible . . . you know—for wishing it on you."

Will's cheeks burned as he glanced back up at Ken. He'd only told him half the story, but Will felt like such an animal for setting Ken up for the fall that he could barely admit the truth to himself, much less to Ken.

"Wow," Ken said, surprise visible in his blue eyes. He stood all the way up as he seemed to process this. "But, well, you made up for it—when you helped us win in the second half."

Will's stomach performed a guilt-ridden somersault. Of course Ken had to go and be all accepting about this, making Will feel like an even worse piece of garbage. "I guess," he said.

Ken shrugged. "Look, we've both done some bad stuff to each other. I just hope it's all in the past."

Will sighed. "Yeah. Me too."

Ken reached out a hand for Will to shake, and Will took it. As they released hands, Ken glanced down at his watch. "Oh, gotta run to practice," he said.

Will nodded. "Go ahead."

Ken turned to walk out, but he paused by the door. "I'm glad we talked," he told Will. Hesitating, he chewed on the inside of his lip. "And, you know, just think about Melissa." Then Ken whipped back around and headed out into the hall.

Will's broad shoulders slumped. Yeah. He was glad they'd talked as well. But Will wasn't going to waste one minute thinking about Melissa. She was a back-stabbing ice queen who wasn't worth his time.

But then, trying to figure out how to erase the past—now, that was something that *was* worth his time, Will thought as he dragged himself out of the chair and onto his crutches.

Because if he could accomplish that, he'd be able to get rid of the moment when he'd arranged for Ken to get hurt. Will swallowed.

And then maybe, just maybe, he could live with himself.

*   *   *

Elizabeth sat at her desk in the *Oracle* office, counting the minutes until their meeting was supposed to start. She glanced down at her silver-link watch and sighed. Why couldn't this day just be over already? Elizabeth's original plan had been to stay in the office after the staff meeting ended and finish some pressing *Oracle* work. But seeing as she was running on empty, that wasn't going to happen today. Elizabeth pushed up the sleeves of her cardigan, her head starting to pound. *Not by a long shot.*

"Hey. Is Megan around?"

Elizabeth bolted up straight, her neck muscles tightening as she heard a familiar male voice. On automatic pilot, she turned around in her metal chair to see Conner talking to Julia McIntyre, a fellow *Oracle* staff member. Elizabeth felt almost frozen in place as she glimpsed Conner, not sure of what to do next. She took in his tall, lean frame, half of her wanting to call out to him. The other half wanted to run again. But this time Elizabeth had nowhere to escape to.

"Not yet," Julia was saying. "She should be here any minute, though."

"Okay. Thanks," Conner responded.

Elizabeth's heart twisted. Still not feeling capable of dealing, she was about to turn around and attempt a magic disappearing act when Conner spotted her, his deep green eyes intensifying. For a brief moment he just stood there and gazed at her, his mouth a straight line. Then, nodding at Elizabeth in greeting, he started to walk over to her.

Meanwhile Elizabeth's heart felt like it was going to pound right out of her rib cage. She gripped her chair's armrests, trying to gain some composure.

"Liz," Conner said. He sat down on the edge of the table in front of her. "Hi."

Elizabeth crossed her legs, then uncrossed them, rubbing her hands up and down against her pants. "Hi," she responded, the word suddenly sounding overwhelmingly silly. "Hi" didn't exactly seem to cover it after all they'd been through.

Conner glanced around the table—at Elizabeth's paperwork and her computer. "Busy?"

Elizabeth blinked. She couldn't believe *this* was the first conversation they were having. Then again, she couldn't think of anything else to talk about either. "Yes." Elizabeth pushed her light blond hair away from her face, desperately searching for something to say. Something to make this exchange at least half normal.

"What about you?" she asked. "I mean, how was your first day back?"

Conner shrugged, then crossed his arms over his chest. "Fine, I guess."

71

Elizabeth slowly nodded, focusing on the partly chewed pencil on her desk, not sure of how to respond to Conner's three-syllable sentence.

"Liz."

Elizabeth glanced back up at him, and her breath practically caught in her throat. He was looking at her with such intensity, such emotion in his eyes. . . . She could almost remember what things used to be like for them.

"It's good to see you," he said, his eyes still trained on hers, his voice gruff.

The longest minute seemed to pass as Elizabeth met Conner's gaze and they just stared at each other, communicating everything with their eyes that they couldn't manage with words. The tiny blond hairs at the base of Elizabeth's neck prickled, and she felt almost incapable of speech. Of thought. Of *anything* other than simply looking at Conner.

"Yeah," Elizabeth responded finally, feeling somewhat shaky. "You too."

Conner leaned forward slightly. He dropped his head for a split second, then looked right at her again, his eyes beyond penetrating. "Liz, I—"

"Hey, there. Heard you were looking for me."

Elizabeth was so startled by the chipper sound of Megan's voice that she nearly jumped out of her seat. Conner stood in a flash and quickly moved his focus from Elizabeth to his sister, who had just stepped up next to them.

"Uh, yeah. Hey," Conner said. He stuffed a hand in his front jeans pocket. "Tell Mom that I'm bringing my guitar in to be tuned. But I'll be home for dinner." Before Megan even had a chance to respond, Conner was already walking away. "Later," he said, giving both Elizabeth and his sister a brief glance, then heading straight for the door.

Elizabeth's heart sank as confusion, annoyance, and hurt swept over her. He laid that heavy moment on her, spinning her emotions in absolute circles, and then he couldn't give her so much as a good-bye directed right at her?

It's like it always is with Conner, Elizabeth thought, slumping into her seat. The thing was, she had kind of hoped that part of him—that unable-to-communicate part—had changed.

Megan dropped down in the chair next to Elizabeth's, wrinkles of confusion popping across her forehead. "What was happening just now?" she asked. "Why'd he leave like that?"

Elizabeth shook her head, letting out a heavy breath. "I don't know," she told her. "I really don't."

Megan looked at Elizabeth for a beat longer, then dropped her green eyes down to her hands. "Guess that's just Conner," she said softly.

73

"Yeah," Elizabeth agreed, sighing. She picked up one of the sheets of paper from the messy pile in front of her and tried to get back to work. But she stared blankly at the paper, then at her computer screen.

Maybe nothing had really changed at all.

Maybe I should be an actor, Andy thought as he and Tia answered the *Test Your Love* producers' questions that afternoon. They were in the same stark interview room they'd been in the day before, sitting in the same folding chairs. Only this time the interview was being taped by a disheveled cameraman, and Mika and Brad were joined by another man and woman, both of whom looked around forty. Aileen, the woman, had black, rectangular-rimmed glasses and long, gray hair that she wore in a ponytail. James, the man sitting next to her, was semibald and a bit chunky.

Andy had no clue what any of the four producers was thinking. All he knew was that he was surprising even himself with his Oscar-worthy performance. *If I did become an actor, that would kind of solve the whole getting-into-a-good-school problem,* he thought, half listening as Tia told the producers the story of their fictional first date. *I wouldn't have to go to college at all.* Then again, if Andy and Tia did get on the game show, that was still a far cry from making big bucks as a star. Skipping out on college probably wouldn't be the best move ever. Andy sat up straight. It couldn't hurt to dream, though, could it?

"All right. We have two more questions for both of you," Aileen announced, pulling Andy out of his fantasies. "Andy, what do you love most about your girlfriend here?"

Andy glanced sideways at Tia and scratched his chin. "Well, let's see, there are so *many* things," he began, causing the producers to let out an exaggerated, "*Awww . . . ,*" and Tia to smile.

Andy grinned. Two more points for him. "But I'd have to say it's her spirit—her energy. She's always up for anything and in such a totally positive way."

Tia leaned over and gave him a kiss on the cheek. "Thanks."

Andy shrugged in response. How ironic. Just when Andy figured out that he was gay, he discovered that he knew all the right things to say to a woman.

"Good answer," Aileen said. She turned her attention to Tia, her hazel eyes widening. "And Tia? What do you love most about Andy?"

"Hands down, his sense of humor," Tia responded, pushing her long, wavy hair behind her shoulder. "He always makes me laugh."

Andy flashed his "girlfriend" a grin. He had to admit that she was also quite a pro at this whole impersonation thing. The two of them made a killer team.

Aileen nodded, marking something down on the legal pad in front of her. "That's definitely important."

Mika leaned forward and chewed on the end of her blue Bic pen. "Here comes the hard one. Andy, what do you like *least* about Tia? What about her just drives you nuts?"

"Remember, buddy. You gotta be honest here," Brad put in.

"Oh, man." Andy tugged at the neckline of his soft cotton shirt as he felt Tia's dark eyes bore into him. *Hopefully she'll remember that this is just an act,* he thought, shifting in his hard metal seat. "Talk about being put on the spot . . . well, okay. The thing is, Tia can be kind of bossy sometimes—"

"That's only because you're so indecisive!" Tia broke in.

So much for remembering it's an act, Andy thought, sinking into his seat.

"Okay, then." Aileen smiled, pushing her glasses on top of her head. "Now we have *both* your answers to that question."

Mika clapped. "You guys are done here. If you go into the waiting area, we'll let you know if you made it in a little while."

"Okay. Thanks," Andy said, standing up.

Tia stood as well, and the two of them were silent as they walked over to the door. *Man. I hope she's not really mad,* Andy thought as they stepped into the hallway. Because hanging out with an angry Tia was *not* a good time. Unfortunately, Andy knew that from firsthand experience.

"I can't believe you said I was *bossy,*" Tia snapped the moment the heavy door slammed behind them.

Andy winced. "Tee, it was part of the act! I was just answering their question. I had to say *something.*"

Tia stared at him with a serious expression a moment longer, then cracked up. "Andy, I'm *kidding,*" she said, nudging him. "That was great in there." She lowered her voice as they walked down the hallway toward the waiting area. "They totally ate it up."

Andy smiled, relieved. "Yeah, yeah, I know. When you said we once broke up because you thought I was flirting with Jessica, that was classic."

Tia pulled her fitted jean jacket off her shoulders, carrying it in her arms. "You had your moments too, my friend."

They reached the waiting room, and eight other couples were already there—Tia and Andy had been among the last to be interviewed today. Andy and Tia glanced around as they stepped inside, noticing that every single couple seemed to be cuddling or cooing at each other in one way or another.

"God. Please tell me that Angel and I were never cheesy like that," Tia whispered as they maneuvered their way around a girl sitting in her boyfriend's lap while she fed him peanuts.

"Never," Andy lied, leading Tia over to the bar area. *Hey.* He'd just narrowly escaped a fight with Tia. He wasn't about to get himself entrenched in another one.

"These couples redefine *cheesy,*" Andy went on, grabbing two glasses off the blue-and-white-tiled bar, then pouring some Coke into them. Still, as he handed Tia her glass, he could tell by the way she was watching the couples look so happy together that she was probably having the same thought as he was—*Being cheesy wouldn't be the* worst *thing....*

"So. You guys survived day two."

Andy's blue eyes widened as Matt, the crew guy from the day before, strolled over. It astounded Andy every time he saw the guy just how good-looking he was. It wasn't fair that someone could look like that when Andy looked like, well, Andy.

"How'd it go?" Matt asked.

"We rocked, of course," Tia responded, smiling coyly. She placed her jean jacket down on the bar and adjusted the straps of her olive green tank sweater.

78

Andy groaned inwardly. If Tia was going to continue with the wide-eyed hair-flipping business, he didn't think he could bear to watch. He'd already pointed out to her that she could kill their chances as "a couple," but there she went anyway, flirting full steam ahead.

Tia leaned onto the bar top and gazed right at Matt. "That camera guy kinda freaked me out, though. I mean, who knows how we'll come off on camera."

Matt looked from Tia to Andy, his hazel eyes crinkling at the corners as he grinned. "I wouldn't worry about that. Somehow I don't think either of you could ever come off badly."

As Andy saw Tia blush out of the corner of his eye, he felt like he could strangle her. This whole thing was her idea, and now she was acting like it didn't matter if they got kicked off the show. *Or who knows,* Andy thought, rolling his eyes. *Maybe something even worse could happen if Tee blows our cover.* Like, maybe they could get arrested for impersonating a couple. *I'd like to see Tee flirt with Matt from behind bars. That would be fun.*

Still, as Andy watched Matt and Tia exchange smiles and flirty looks, he had to admit that Tia risking their chances wasn't what was *really* bothering him about this whole scene.

Andy sighed, stepping away from Romeo and Juliet to go sit in the plaid overstuffed armchair by the big-screen TV. What was actually getting to him was that Tia could moan and groan all she wanted to about how hard it was to meet guys, but the truth was—comparatively—she had it easy. Come to think of it, so did all of Andy's other friends and all the other people in this room.

All they had to accomplish was meeting the right person. Then they could simply take it from there.

Andy looked down at the ground as the soap-opera couple on the television screen began to kiss passionately. He kicked at the carpet.

Andy, on the other hand, didn't even know where to begin.

Will Simmons

I have to admit, I was wrong about Ken Matthews. I was a total jerk to want to try to take him down. I mean, the way Ken came up to me and apologized to me, actually said what he said, shows that he has to be a stand-up guy. No question.

But I learned something else about Ken today too. The fact that he thinks Melissa and I should get back together!

Well, let's just say he's not the smartest guy in Sweet Valley.

CHAPTER
Lowest of the Low

6

What a practice, Ken thought as he rubbed his over-worked shoulder, trying to get out a throbbing ache. The football team's physical practice had just come to an end, and Coach Riley had run them ragged. Now the guys were all sitting on the wooden bleachers as Coach went over some plays with them.

Ken wiped the sweat off his forehead as he listened, feeling totally exhausted. But exhausted in a pumped-up, worked-hard, adrenaline-high *good* way. Coach cleared his throat, and Ken glanced up at the cloudless blue sky for a moment, letting out a heavy breath. He was also feeling good because of that conversation he'd had with Will earlier. Approaching the guy had been one of the hardest things Ken had ever done, but it had turned out to be well worth it. Now they could both move past those bad feelings and get on with their lives. And maybe, just maybe, he had gotten through to Will on the Melissa issue. Ken pulled at his gray T-shirt, air-

82

ing out his damp chest. Yep. Hopefully that good karma would start rolling his way about now.

"We need to talk about the pep rally," Coach Riley announced, clapping his stubby hands. "We're going to get the whole school psyched up for the final play-off game, *right?*"

"Right!" Ken shouted back along with his fellow teammates, their voices reverberating across the field. Ken smiled slightly to himself. It was moments like these that he felt how glad he was to be part of a team again. There was nothing else like it.

Coach Riley crossed his arms over his rather bulky chest. "All right, then. The rally's going to be on Friday. Tradition calls for the captain to plan the thing out with the head cheerleader." Coach dropped his arms by his sides and zeroed in on Ken. "Matthews— with Simmons still out, this falls on you. Okay?"

Ken nodded, sliding forward on the bleacher. "Yeah. Of course, Coach."

Coach pointed at him, his brown eyes opened wide. "Remember, this rally has to be huge. *Huge*— all right?"

"No problem," Ken said, wiping his damp hands against his blue cotton shorts. "You got it."

"Good." Coach moved his eyes off Ken, taking in the whole team. "Practice is over, everyone. See you tomorrow."

Ken had stood and was stretching out his legs, already trying to think of ideas for the rally, when he heard Josh Radinsky behind him mutter, "That's so wrong. Will should be the one planning this thing."

"No kidding," Matt Wells responded. "What's Coach thinking? It's not like Simmons's injury would get in the way of *that*."

"Yeah," Jake Collins agreed. "Will was captain all season. Ken's been stand-in captain for two minutes."

Ken's neck muscles tightened as his face began to flush. He quickly jogged down the rest of the bleachers, not wanting to hear what any of the other guys had to say. It only made him feel like the lowest of the low. Ken stomped across the field, his hands balling into fists.

The thing was, Ken would offer to pass the job on to Will, but he wasn't sure that Coach Riley would appreciate it. Besides, Ken was pretty certain that he knew exactly why Coach had given this task to him instead of to Will—because it might not be a good idea to ask Will to plan a pep rally for a game he wouldn't even play in. It could end up bumming Will out.

Ken kicked at a twig as he headed toward the locker-room doors. Knowing that Coach was on his side didn't make him feel much better, though. Because that feeling-like-part-of-a-team stuff?

All of that was pretty much shot to pieces.

"All right, girls, I know it's late, so I'll make this quick," Coach Laufeld told the group of cheerleaders sitting in a half circle before her as practice came to an end on Monday afternoon.

Melissa let out a short breath of relief. Her head was pounding, she was hungry, and she felt weak. She pulled the red elastic out of her ponytail, letting her long, brown hair fall against her back. All she wanted to do was go home.

"As you know, there will be a big pep rally on Friday to gear up for the final play-off game." Coach Laufeld slipped her hands in the pockets of her red sweatpants. "Now, normally I assign the head cheerleader to work with the football captain to plan the rally, but seeing as Tia went home sick today, I'm going to have to select someone else."

"But Coach, I'm sure she'll be feeling better tomorrow," Jessica, sitting diagonally across from Melissa, put in. Coach Laufeld raised her eyebrows at the statement, and Jessica added, "I mean, she's not majorly sick or anything." Flushing slightly, Jessica bit her lip. "Of course she *was* sick enough to have to go home, but—"

"Enough, Jessica," Coach Laufeld interrupted, shaking her head. "The point is it's important to have someone responsible in charge of this event. And since we can't really rely on Tia at the moment, I'm going to ask Melissa to take over."

Melissa's light blue eyes widened. "Me?" she asked, excitement building in her stomach.

"Yes. Unless you're not up for it."

"No, no, of course I am," Melissa responded quickly, smiling.

Coach Laufeld nodded, her brown ponytail bouncing up and down. "Good. We'll talk details later. Now, I have one more thing to go over with you guys. . . ."

Cherie Reese, who was sitting next to Melissa, gave her a little nudge of support, and Melissa lost track of what Coach was saying, reveling in the moment instead. To begin with, she couldn't help but shoot Jessica a look of triumph—a look that Jessica pointedly chose to ignore. But whatever. Melissa still knew in her heart that she deserved to be head cheerleader, and the fact that Coach Laufeld had chosen her to plan the pep rally only proved that.

Melissa glanced down and played with the soft silver chain bracelet that hung off her slender wrist. Finally she was starting to get what was hers. And if she was supposed to plan this thing with Will, well, then maybe—

Melissa broke her thought, her mouth falling slightly open as she realized that Will wasn't technically football captain at the moment. *Ken is,* she realized, her stomach turning over. Of course, there was still a chance that Coach Riley would ask Will to plan the pep rally. But just the thought that Ken might be the person Melissa had to work with created such anger in her, caused so much nausea to wash over her, that she wasn't sure taking the position from Tia was even worth it.

All of the muscles in Melissa's body suddenly felt tense as Coach Laufeld dismissed them.

"See?" Gina Cho said, her stick-straight dark hair falling over her face as she leaned in to whisper to Melissa. "You should've been head cheerleader all along."

Melissa smiled, her muscles relaxing. Who was she kidding? Of course it was worth it.

Tia sat in a purple armchair next to Andy in *Test Your Love*'s waiting area, staring blankly at the big-screen TV before her. *Hollywood Scoop* was on, but she barely registered the pieces of gossip the frosty-haired host was excitedly reporting. Tia was too busy being nervous to concentrate.

She pulled her short legs up onto the chair and crossed them Indian style, playing with the cuff of her black pants. The problem was, Tia had revised the whole not-wanting-to-get-on-the-show-because-of-Matt issue. Now Tia *really* wanted to be on *Test Your Love* more than ever. It would be so much fun to be a contestant, and Tia got totally psyched up every time she thought of the possibility that she and Andy could win a trip to New York.

Tia chewed on the inside of her mouth as anxious butterflies began to flutter around in her stomach. Plus she had also reasoned that if they did make the show, she would get another chance to see Matt. It was so obvious the guy was into her—he didn't even seem to care that she had a boyfriend. *I'm sure he'd ask me out once we finished taping,* Tia thought, smiling to herself.

"Hey. What are you thinking about?" Andy asked, leaning toward her.

Tia turned to look at him. She attempted a casual shrug. "Nothing, really," she lied. She didn't feel like hearing another one of Andy's don't-flirt-with-the-crew lectures. They had gotten completely boring already.

"Really?" Andy asked, arching a red-blond eyebrow. "All *I* can think about is making the show."

Tia rolled her eyes and pulled down on her tank

sweater. "Well, I'm trying not to, okay? I'm nervous enough as it is."

Andy gave her a lopsided smile. "That's classic Tee. You don't get the least bit nervous for a calc exam, but you get all wigged out about making some game show."

Tia couldn't help but smile at that, but the grin disappeared in a flash. *I am completely wigged out,* she realized. Her knees now seemed to be bouncing on their own. *Relax. It's just television,* she told herself, but that only caused the wave of flutters in her stomach to intensify tenfold.

"Can we talk about something else?" she asked Andy, clasping his skinny arm. "Please? *Anything* else?"

Andy let out a short laugh but then nodded. "Yeah, okay," he said. "Well . . . did you see Conner today at school? He seemed pretty good, didn't he?"

"Yes. He did," she agreed, suddenly feeling like a candidate for Most Selfish Friend. One of her best friends had just come home from rehab, and she wasn't even thinking about him? Instead she was getting all caught up in auditioning for a game show? *I'm totally horrible,* Tia thought, her stomach sinking. *Could I be any more shallow?*

Then she had an idea—one that made her brighten a bit. "We should do something for

Conner—you know, welcome him home. Show him we care."

"Like what?"

"Like . . . throw him a surprise party." Tia's eyes widened. "Yeah, that's it. A surprise party. That's totally what we should do." She hugged herself, starting to get excited about the prospect. "We could get his mom in on it and—"

"Um, Tee?" Andy cut in. Closing her mouth, Tia stopped talking and looked at him. "Hate to burst your bubble, but do you really think *Conner* would want a surprise party? That's not really his type of thing, if you know what I mean."

Tia's face fell. She *did* know what he meant. Conner was all about being cool and removed and guarded. Party favors and sweet sentiments weren't what he was into. Then again, Conner *was* into parties. And even though Tia knew he would never admit it in a trillion years, Conner would definitely be touched that his friends would put in such an effort to show their support.

"Okay, so we'll make sure the whole thing has a mellow vibe," Tia reasoned. "And there won't be any elements of corniness anywhere."

"Definitely." Andy nodded, crossing his arms over his chest. "If we're going to do this, the corn factor has to be zilch. Nada."

Tia raised her eyebrows, the corners of her mouth forming into a smile. "Does that mean you're gonna help me plan this thing?"

"Hey." Andy shrugged. "I'm your boyfriend. I gotta help you with things like this, right?"

Tia almost laughed. But Andy's use of the word *boyfriend* caused her nervousness to hit her with full force again, making laughter impossible. Instead she paled.

"Um, I was only kidding," Andy whispered, leaning forward. "I don't *really* think I'm your boyfriend."

But before Tia could respond, a jarring silence overtook the room. The TV was clicked off. Tia glanced over her shoulder and saw that Mika was standing in the doorway. Tia shot Andy a quick, worried look, then swallowed, turning all the way around.

Just let us make this thing, she thought, crossing fingers on both hands. *That's all I ask—* Tia spotted Matt standing in the corner of the room, looking sexy as ever. She bit her lip. *Well, that's not all I ask, but—* Tia shook her head, trying to clear her head. *Whatever. Just let us make this thing, all right?*

"Okay, okay," Mika began. "I'll start by saying you guys are all great—and I hate you all for being such happy couples." Some nervous laughs broke out across the room. "But unfortunately, we could only pick three couples. So here goes."

Mika glanced down at her clipboard, and Tia grasped the cushy edges of the chair, closing her eyes. *Just let us make this thing. That's all I ask.* Really.

"Couple one—Marsden and Ramirez," Mika announced.

Tia's eyes flew open. Matt was the first person she saw—he was giving her a thumbs-up from across the room. Smiling from ear to ear, Tia jumped up and was almost knocked over by Andy, who had just jumped up as well.

"All right, Tee!" Andy exclaimed, giving her a big, hearty hug. "We did it! We're gonna be on TV."

Tia hugged him back, her heart racing. "I know, I know!" she yelled out. She paused, staring at Andy for a second. She was so happy right now, she really could kiss her fake boyfriend.

Tia shook her head. *Why not,* she thought, throwing her arms around Andy's neck.

And then she promptly kissed him.

To: marsden1@swiftnet.com
From: tee@swiftnet.com
Subject: the party

andy,
   I spoke to conner's mom. she's up
for the party and said we can throw
it at her house. we'll talk details
later.
   can u believe we're going to be on
tv? you better be studying your tia
factoids!
                         love,
                         tee

To: tee@swiftnet.com
From: marsden1@swiftnet.com
Subject: re: the party

Tee,
   I have five words for you:
   Don't ever kiss me again.
                    Andy

CHAPTER
Baggage-Free

7

"I hope pork chops are okay," Mrs. Sandborn said to Conner that evening as she placed a pink-rimmed plate filled with a chop, a mound of rice, and some broccoli down in front of him. "I know it's not the usual, but, well, I'm making an attempt at variety."

Conner glanced up at his mom, taking in the flash of tentativeness in her blue eyes. Ever since he'd come home yesterday, she'd been trying so hard that she almost seemed anxious. Uneasy. *Kind of how she was when* she *came home from rehab*, Conner thought.

"Chops are cool," he told her, trying hard to keep any trace of annoyance out of his voice. If there was one lesson Conner had learned these past several weeks, it was that as difficult as it was to believe sometimes, he actually had more things in his life to be grateful for than to be bitter about. Conner took a bite of rice. His family was definitely one of those things.

"Did you get your guitar fixed?" asked Megan, who was sitting across from him.

Conner reached for the bowl of applesauce, spooning some onto his pork. "Yeah."

Megan regarded him with wide green eyes. "You know, you kinda left the *Oracle* in a hurry."

Conner dropped the spoon back in the ceramic applesauce bowl, making a clanging noise. He averted his eyes from Megan down to his plate. When his sister was nosy like that, it was a bit harder for Conner to remember that he was grateful for her. "Yeah." He scratched the back of his neck. "Well, I had to go."

Conner felt Megan's eyes linger on him a moment longer, but he ignored her, cutting into his pork chop. He felt bad enough about that scene at the *Oracle* office as it was. He didn't need his sister's questions on top of it. Conner was well aware of the fact that he probably bummed Elizabeth out, ditching her the way he had this afternoon. And man, she was the very last person he wanted to upset. But Conner just didn't know how to deal. All he wanted to do when he saw Elizabeth—the very first moment he saw her—was grab her and kiss her and tell her how much she meant to him. How much he appreciated her. She was one of the major reasons he was able to get clean. He thought about her a lot. *All the time,* Conner thought, swallowing.

Putting down his knife and fork, Conner stared

95

down at his plate. The problem was, Conner knew he didn't deserve Elizabeth. Not after what he put her through when he was drinking. Conner's stomach formed into a tight knot. *And not after what happened in rehab,* he thought, shifting in his wooden, straight-back seat.

"Conner? Are you all right?" Mrs. Sandborn asked. "You don't like the pork chops?"

Conner looked over at his mom, then down at his barely touched plate. "No, it's good. I'm just not that hungry."

"You sure?" Mrs. Sandborn asked, fingering her short strand of pink pearls. "Because I can get you something else."

"No. Don't," Conner responded, now using all of his effort not to sound irritated. "I like the pork." And then, just to stop her from looking at him *like that,* he took another bite of his dinner.

The phone rang, and Megan immediately stood up. "I'll get it," she said, hurrying over to the wall-mounted phone in the kitchen.

"So, things went okay at school today?" Mrs. Sandborn asked. She was clearly trying to adopt a casual tone, but Conner wasn't fooled. For one, she had already asked him this question. *Twice.*

Conner slumped back into his seat, wondering if this was how it was going to be from now on, his mom acting supercautious around him at all times. Still, Conner realized that he didn't really have a right to be defensive. After all, when his mom had come home from rehab, Conner was just waiting for her to hit the gin bottle. He'd expected it.

"Yeah. Everything went fine," Conner told her for the third time that evening.

"It's for you," Megan said, walking over to Conner, her eyebrows all scrunched together. "Someone named Alanna?"

Conner's stomach suddenly felt hollowed out and empty. *Alanna.* His neck and shoulder muscles tensed. What was she doing calling him here? Now?

He gripped the blue-and-white-checked handle of his knife. "Tell her I'm not home."

"But Conner, I just tol—"

"Tell her I'm not home," Conner repeated, glancing away from his sister.

"Oo-kay," she said, then jogged off to pick up the phone again.

"Who's Alanna?" Mrs. Sandborn asked. "Is she in one of your classes?"

"Yeah. Sort of," Conner lied, wanting to put a swift end to his mother's questions.

But Megan wasn't going to let the subject rest. "Who is she?" Megan asked as soon as she returned to the table. "Why didn't you want to talk to her?"

97

Conner sighed. "She's no one," he said, pushing the rice around on his plate. "And I didn't want to talk because I'm in the middle of eating dinner."

"But I could've told her that," Megan countered, picking up her glass of water. "I didn't have to say that you weren't here."

Conner gave Megan an even stare. "Sandy, just drop it. All right?"

Megan's light eyes widened as she sipped her water. "Fine." Placing her glass down on the oak table, she threw up her hands as if she was surrendering. "It's dropped."

Conner was silent. He stared back down at his picked-at dinner, his neck and shoulder muscles more tense than ever. Not only did he not want to talk about Alanna, he didn't want to think about her. Because when he did, he was reminded of what they had.

Conner's stomach twisted. And of why he could never get back together with Elizabeth.

Melissa was a big believer in fate. In her mind, everyone controlled their own destinies. Being successful in life was a matter of taking things into your own hands. And on Tuesday morning that was exactly what she intended to do.

Melissa smiled slightly to herself as she pulled

her history textbook out of her locker and stuffed it into her brown leather backpack. She was beginning to feel that her own life was heading for an upswing—and simply because she deserved it. After all, the reason Coach Laufeld had selected Melissa to plan the pep rally was directly due to Melissa's hard work on the squad. And when Melissa had come home last night, her mother didn't get on her case for once.

Finally, Melissa thought, fastening the silver buckles on her backpack. She swung her bag over her shoulder and glanced at her reflection in the rectangular mirror that hung on the inside of her locker door, making sure that her hair looked in order and that her sheer lip gloss was still on. And as she reached into the small front pocket of her bag to pull out the pink tube of gloss to reapply, she was thinking that while Ken was clearly an idiot, he was right about one thing—Will did seem like he was starting to get his act together again. And if Will and Melissa were both experiencing an upswing at the same time, then maybe—

Melissa's eyes widened. At that very moment Will walked right by her on his crutches, obviously heading for his locker on the other side of the hall. Melissa quickly closed the tube of gloss and put it back in her bag, shutting her locker door. Of course, she didn't believe in signs or any garbage like that. But if she *did* . . . well, Will passing right by her at the exact moment she was thinking about him was a sign if she ever heard of one.

Melissa adjusted her short, gray skirt and headed straight for locker number eighty-three—Will's locker.

But as Melissa neared Will's toned back, her confidence suddenly wavered a bit, her knees feeling like jelly. She hesitated for a moment, fidgeting with the gold ring on her left hand. She didn't really think she could handle it if Will didn't want to talk to her. Which was completely possible. He'd blasted her after the game Friday night.

Melissa shook her head. *This is* Will, she told herself. *No one knows you better. He was in love with you for years. He has to still care.* Melissa tilted up her chin and walked over to him. He didn't seem to notice her standing there, and she was silent for a moment as she watched him turn the combination on his lock.

24, 13, 37 . . . Melissa bit her lip. How many times had she watched him open that lock in the past? How many times had *she* opened it? She swallowed. "Hi," she said softly, looking at his profile.

Will's shoulders visibly tightened. He clicked his lock and swung open his locker door without saying a word, without even looking up at her.

Melissa's knees started to weaken again, but she

ignored it, focusing all of her energy on Will. *Just make him remember,* she told herself. *Remember what we were like.* She glanced at the green button-down shirt he was wearing and realized that *she* had given it to him for Christmas last year.

"I just wanted to congratulate you again," Melissa offered, pushing a strand of her long hair behind her ear. "It was because of you that we won the game on Friday. I hope you know that."

Will closed his eyes and dropped his head, letting out a half sigh, half laugh. Then, lifting his head, he looked right at Melissa, his eyes accusing. "How stupid do you think I am?" he snapped, his cheeks turning pink.

Melissa's stomach did a somersault. She felt all the color drain from her already pale face. "Will, I—"

"Just shut up, Melissa," Will interrupted, his knuckles whitening as he gripped the handle of one of his crutches.

Melissa blinked, stung. She couldn't even speak. She could barely *see.*

"I *know* that Ken dumped you, okay? And I also know that's the only reason you're talking to me right now." Will shook his head. "God, Liss, you're so freakin' predictable," he said under his breath. He turned back to his locker and began to pull out some books.

Melissa stared at Will as a tight ball rose in her throat, trying to process the accusations he'd just thrown at her. She felt like she could faint. Or throw up. Or both. She opened her mouth to speak but then closed it as she realized she had no idea what to say.

Stunned, Melissa was about to slump away when it hit her with full force that this wasn't fair. *He pushes me away—basically pushes me right into Ken's arms—and I'm the one who's wrong?* Melissa crossed her arms over her chest, her eyes watering a little as she absorbed the fact that the former love of her life, the guy she used to count on for just about anything, could speak to her with such venom.

"Will, the *reason* I'm talking to you right now is because I wanted to show my support," Melissa said in a measured voice. "You can read whatever you want into it, but that's all there is. It's simple."

Will shut his locker door and turned to look at her, his expression slightly softer.

"I care about you," Melissa added.

Will met her eyes—*really* met her eyes—for what seemed like the first time in weeks. His square jaw unclenched a bit, and his mouth relaxed. He looked like he was beginning to back down. Melissa's lips parted slightly. Maybe, just maybe, *her* Will was back. . . .

"Melissa, the only person you care about is yourself." Will turned around on his crutches and didn't glance back as he hobbled off.

Melissa stared after Will, feeling like he'd just

socked her in the stomach. Which she'd actually prefer to the emotional pain she was experiencing right now.

Melissa dropped her arms by her sides, her eyes welling up with tears. If Will *had* knocked her out, at least she'd be unconscious.

Which would be a better feeling than having her heart ripped to pieces.

Evan felt a little silly as he waited by Jade's locker before third period that morning. Knowing a girl's schedule and trying to steal five minutes with her seemed like such a teenybopper, *Dawson's Creek*-esque thing to do. Which was *not* Evan's style.

Evan's style usually consisted of the more straightforward approach—calling a girl up, hanging out with her, and telling her exactly how he felt. But Jade was different somehow. He couldn't help feeling that a flirty, kind of romantic tactic would suit Jade better. Evan swallowed, running a hand through his long, black hair. The problem was, Evan wasn't a flirty kind of guy. Which made him wonder whether or not he and Jade were really a good match.

But then Evan moved out of the way so that a freckle-faced girl could get to her locker, and he spotted Jade coming down the hall. *Scratch that last thought.* Jade couldn't be a better match for him. *Except for the fact that she's way too beautiful,* Evan thought, taking in the way her silky, straight hair swung as she walked and how her dark, almond-shaped eyes sparkled as she smiled at him. Jade was also the cutest, most unique dresser around. Today she looked amazing in a black tank top with a short, bright orange flare skirt, black tights, and black Mary Jane–type shoes. Evan grinned back at her. Jade was definitely one of the coolest girls in Sweet Valley.

"Waiting for me?" Jade asked as she reached him, arching one dark eyebrow.

Evan leaned against the locker next to Jade's. "Just happened to be in the right place at the right time."

Jade nodded, still smiling as she turned to open her locker. "I see. Lucky for you."

Evan laughed, realizing he didn't care if all of this flirting was a little on the teenybopper side. After all, *this* was how a relationship was supposed to start out—baggage-free and based on a solid friendship. So a little flirting couldn't hurt, could it?

Evan had leaned in a bit, about to respond to Jade's remark, when Tia passed by, stopping in place as soon as she spotted Evan. She turned on her heel and strolled right toward him.

"Evan," Tia said. "Just the man I was looking for."

Evan stood up straight and crossed his arms over his chest. "What's up?"

"Just wanted to tell you that we're throwing a

surprise welcome-home party for Conner tomorrow night."

Evan blinked. "A surprise party? For *Conner?*"

Tia let out a dramatic sigh. "I know, I know, Conner won't want a surprise party, yada, yada, yada."

"Well, yeah," Evan responded. "Exactly."

Tia shook her head. "Don't worry about it. The party's gonna be a totally mellow, laid-back thing. Conner will like it. Trust me." She shifted her backpack from her left shoulder to her right one. "So, tomorrow night. Eight o'clock. Andy's house. Okay?"

Evan shrugged. If Tia was going to take responsibility for this, there wasn't much he could say. "Yeah. Okay."

Tia turned to go but grabbed Jade's arm before walking off. "Oh, and you're welcome too. The more it's like a regular party with lots of people there, the happier Conner'll be. So come, all right?"

"Sure," Jade said, pulling down on the hem of her tank top. "I'll be there."

"Cool." Tia flashed her a smile, then headed off down the hall.

Jade looked at Evan. "Looks like we'll get to hang out tomorrow night," she commented, toying with the silver oval pendant that dangled off her necklace.

"Yeah," Evan responded, suddenly unable to take his eyes off Jade's sexy collarbone. "But what about this afternoon?" When Jade raised her eyebrows, he added, "I mean, are you gonna come to my swim meet?"

The corners of Jade's mouth formed into a smile. She widened her dark eyes. "Do you *want* me to come?" she asked in a teasing voice.

Evan grinned, falling in step with Jade as they both started to walk toward their next class. "I don't know," he said, playing along. "Do you want me to want you to come?"

Jade's eyes flashed with amusement as they neared her classroom's door. "You're supposed to be able to figure that out, you know."

"Ah. I see." Evan stopped walking. He glanced down at the old industrial carpeting and then back up at Jade. "Well, I'm going to take a wild stab in the dark and say yes, I want you to come."

Jade flipped her hair behind her shoulder. "Very good. Right answer." The first bell rang, and Jade started to turn to head into her class. She paused, poking Evan. "Cute panda, by the way," she said, referring to the picture of the animal on his T-shirt. Then she ducked into her classroom.

Evan smiled to himself, his skin tingling from Jade's touch as he jogged off to make it to class. He had come to a definitive conclusion, he decided, hanging a left at the end of the hall.

A little flirting *definitely* couldn't hurt.

Jade Wu

DATE BOOK

<u>Monday</u>:
   4:00 Cheerleading practice.
   8:00 Study for French quiz. Work on history paper.

<u>Tuesday</u>:
   4:00 Cheerleading canceled. Go to Evan's swim meet.
   7:00 Meet Mom at home for dinner.
   8:00 Finish history paper. Start book for English.

<u>Wednesday</u>:
   4:00 Cheerleading practice.
   8:00 Go to Conner's party with Evan.

<u>Thursday</u>:
   4:00 Cheerleading practice.

<u>Friday</u>:
   Pep rally.
   8:00 Go to the movies with Evan?

<u>Saturday</u>:
   Do something with Evan?

Okay, I'm noticing a theme here. . . .

CHAPTER

Ms. Sweetness Routine

8

"So, Gina says that Christi Jacobs has been telling *everyone* that she has some hot boyfriend at Big Mesa, but apparently she made him up! Can you believe it?" Cherie asked, twirling a strand of her red hair around her finger.

Melissa sighed. "Yes, I can," she responded as she and Cherie walked around a huddle of juniors talking in the middle of the hall. "We already know the girl is pathetic."

Sometimes Melissa really wished she could put her friendships on hold. Just drop her friends when they became, well, irritating and come back to them when they were easier to deal with. Cherie, for example, was one of Melissa's oldest friends. But right now the girl was giving her a splitting headache.

"Well, yeah. But inventing a boyfriend? That's, like, beyond lame," Cherie pointed out. She pulled a small tub of lip balm out of her black pants pocket. "Oh! And you won't believe what Josh Radinsky told me about Max Winters," she went on, applying some of the balm to her full lips. "He said . . ."

Melissa briefly froze in place as Cherie continued on with her story. She wasn't particularly interested in what Cherie had to say in the first place, but even more important, there was something going on at the end of the hall that demanded Melissa's full attention.

She began to slowly walk, her shoulders stiffening and her clear blue eyes narrowing as she took in the scene. A very distasteful scene. Ken was in the process of walking over to Maria. Melissa stopped in place again, crossing her arms over her chest. In fact, now Ken had reached his ex-girlfriend and was starting up a conversation with her.

We've been broken up for four days, and he's already chasing after his ex? Melissa thought, her stomach muscles twisting as she took in the way Ken was smiling at Maria. And then it struck her. Ken had only encouraged Melissa to get back with Will so that he'd feel okay about pursuing Maria.

Well. Melissa dropped her arms by her sides, her manicured hands forming into fists. She'd take care of *that*.

"So," Cherie said, oblivious of the minidrama that was playing out right in front of her. "Isn't he total scum?"

"Yes," Melissa said, not taking her glare off Ken and Maria. "Yes, he is."

How could I have ever let Maria go? Ken wondered as he listened to his ex-girlfriend talk, taking in her dark, sparkling eyes, her smooth skin, and the short, shining curls that framed her delicate face. For now, he should probably just be grateful that she hadn't run away when he approached her in the hall and said hi a minute ago.

"So . . . how's your sister doing?" Ken asked, fidgeting with the hem of his worn-out red T-shirt.

"Oh. Great, of course," Maria responded. She glanced down at her hands, twisting the thick silver band that she always wore around her middle finger. She let out a small sigh. "Excelling as always."

Ken shook his head. He could never understand why someone as gorgeous and brilliant as Maria was constantly comparing herself to her older sister—and coming up short. "Yeah, well, that runs in the family."

Maria glanced back up and smiled slightly, which just about melted Ken's heart. How could he have believed that he didn't want her back? That he wanted *Melissa* instead?

"What about you?" she asked, leaning her tall, slender body up against the row of lockers. "How are things with your dad?"

Now it was Ken's turn to glance down. He kicked at a stray pencil on the ground. "Not horrible. Not great." He shrugged and looked back up at Maria. "The same, I guess."

Maria crossed her arms over her chest. "Sorry," she said. "But it takes time for stuff like that. I'm sure you'll work things out."

"I hope so," Ken said. Unbelievable. She was always so optimistic. In fact, that was one of the things Ken loved most about Maria. Unlike Melissa, who was one of the most pessimistic people in southern California.

Speak of the devil . . . Ken glanced to his right and saw that Melissa herself was marching right toward him. And she was . . . *smiling brightly?*

"Ken, hi, I've been looking all over for you," Melissa announced in a saccharine voice. Pushing her dark brown hair behind her ear, she reached over and picked a piece of imaginary lint off Ken's broad shoulder. "We have some important things to discuss, you know."

Ken squinted at Melissa, trying to figure out where this Ms. Sweetness routine was coming from, especially after she'd made it clear yesterday that she basically considered him to be evil incarnate.

Ken shifted his weight from one foot to the other. "Melissa, what—"

"I've gotta go," Maria suddenly broke in. Her dark eyes had lost any trace of warmth. Before Ken could say anything more, she hurried off, her curls bouncing as she walked.

As Ken watched Maria disappear into the pre-lunch swarms crowding the hallway, then glanced back and took in Melissa's self-satisfied smirk, he realized what was going on. *She put on that act on purpose,* Ken thought, clenching his teeth. *Just so Maria would think we're still together and stalk off the way she did.*

Ken felt his face heat up as he met Melissa's now cold gaze. If she wasn't a girl, and if Ken didn't think that she still had somewhat of a right to be bitter, he really could've hit her. "What? What's so important?" he demanded.

Melissa's eyes widened, all innocence. "Planning the pep rally. You do think that's important, don't you?"

Ken rolled his eyes. It was all he could do not to pick Melissa up and shake her with frustration. "Of course. But I'm planning the thing with Tia. You don't need to worry about it."

"But I do," Melissa countered. She glanced down, pressing out the creases of her gray skirt. "Tia wasn't at practice yesterday, so Coach assigned me to the job."

Ken blinked. "Wait a minute," he said, his stomach

112

turning over. "You mean *we're* going to plan the rally? *Together?*"

Melissa glared at him, her mouth a straight line. "I'm not happy about it either, okay? But we don't have a choice. So let's just get it over with. When do you want to meet to talk about it?"

Ken licked his lips as he tried to wrap his brain around the fact that this was actually happening. If he wasn't in the situation himself, he might have even thought it was funny. After all, there was no way he and Melissa would be able to communicate well enough to plan a meal, much less a major event. Ken swallowed, his mind reeling. *This is going to be the saddest pep rally in the history of Sweet Valley High,* he thought, his palms starting to sweat.

"Ken? Hello?" Melissa prodded. She looked down at her silver-and-gold watch. "I don't have all day. Is tomorrow night good for you?"

Ken had opened his mouth to respond when something Melissa had said earlier suddenly struck him. *We don't have a choice.* The way he saw it, they *did* have a choice. After all, if Coach Laufeld had replaced Tia with Melissa, then the football team could switch their choice for rally planner as well—right? Ken would be killing two birds with one stone. *The rest of the team thought Will should be in charge anyway,* he told himself. *So what's the harm? And if the*

113

time alone brings Will and Melissa closer, that would just be a bonus.

"Ken," Melissa cut into his thoughts. "Today."

"Um, yeah, right," Ken responded, cracking his knuckles as he worked out the beginnings of a plan. "Tomorrow's fine. How about seven-thirty—House of Java?"

"Fine," Melissa responded crisply. "Don't be late." And with that, she turned on her heel and stalked off.

Ken cracked his knuckles again, thinking that he had to find Will. *Fast.* His own mental health depended on it.

"Hey, Liz."

Elizabeth let out a little gasp at the sudden sound of the male voice behind her. She jolted forward, nearly spilling her vegetable soup all over the skinny freshman who was ahead of her in the cafeteria line. Setting her orange plastic tray down on the metal counter, Elizabeth turned around, holding a hand to her heart as she glimpsed Evan standing there.

"You scared me," she said, her cheeks flushing.

"Yeah, I get that," Evan responded. He leaned forward to grab a plastic-wrapped peanut-butter-and-jelly sandwich from the rows displayed before him. "Sorry. Didn't mean to."

Elizabeth shook her head, taking a step as the line moved slowly along. "It's probably my fault. I've been kinda on edge lately."

"Still a little freaked about seeing Conner?" Evan asked, his voice soft.

Elizabeth bit her lip. That was the understatement of the year. Sighing, she pushed a strand of her shoulder-length hair behind her ear. "Yes. I guess so," she admitted as they got to the salad bar.

Evan was silent. Elizabeth reached over and grabbed some of the wilted iceberg lettuce out of a big gray vat with a pair of metal tongs, dumping the salad into a little wooden bowl. Moving on to the selection of salad dressings, she frowned as she noticed that something was floating in the neon orange French dressing. Her stomach turning, she opted for the oil and vinegar.

"You know, I'm feeling a little guilty that we haven't said anything to him yet," Evan said.

Elizabeth glanced up from her sorry-looking salad.

"I mean, about us," he added.

Elizabeth grasped the grooved edges of the tray, her mood sinking rapidly. Her heart twisted as she realized that Conner hadn't even given her the opportunity to tell him about Evan . . . or anything at all, for that matter.

115

"I know," Elizabeth said. "Me too. But when you think about it, we didn't really do anything wrong— nothing happened between us until after Conner broke up with me."

Evan stepped up next to Elizabeth as they neared the end of the line. "Yeah, I guess. But as his friend, I still never should've gone after you."

Elizabeth's cheeks burned as she completed that sentence in her head. *And I never should've gone after you.* She stared at her lunch, suddenly not the least bit hungry. "I'll tell him when the time's right," she said. And she would. That was, if Conner didn't keep running from her like the plague.

"Good, because—"

"Hey, there." Jade strolled over at that moment, interrupting Evan midsentence. She smiled at him, but when she noticed that he was talking with Elizabeth, she stiffened a bit.

"Hey to you," Evan said, grinning back at her.

Jade made a show of giving Evan a kiss on the cheek. "Just wanted to tell you that I have a table in the corner," she said, clearly leaving Elizabeth out of the invitation.

She's jealous, Elizabeth realized, noticing the way Jade was self-consciously looking from Evan to Elizabeth and back again. Jade felt threatened by what she had meant to Evan. And for a brief moment

116

Elizabeth felt a twinge of satisfaction. But then she quickly got angry with herself. *You* don't *mean anything to Evan anymore. Not like that.*

"Oh, hey, I might be a little late for Conner's party," Jade went on to Evan as the three of them started to head toward the seating section of the cafeteria. "I have to work tomorrow."

Elizabeth stopped in place. "Party?" she repeated, totally confused. "What party?" If Jade was going to say that *Conner* was throwing a party, Elizabeth was prepared to just pack up and leave Sweet Valley altogether.

"Didn't Tee tell you?" Evan asked. "She's throwing Conner this surprise, welcome-home thing."

Elizabeth blinked, her stomach muscles knotting. "She is?"

Evan shook his head. "I know, I know. He's gonna hate it. I already tried to talk her out of it, but Tia's all gung ho." Evan let out a snort. "I think all of this game-show business is draining the girl of her sanity."

"Oh," Elizabeth said, even though Conner's reaction was the furthest thing from her mind. What *was* on her mind was the fact that she didn't like being the last one to know about his party. She was sure that she was invited—she simply hadn't seen Tia yet today. But still. It felt strange. Even Jade knew about the bash before Elizabeth did. *If this were six weeks ago, I'd be the one* throwing *the party,* Elizabeth thought, her brain reeling.

Then again, what was she thinking? Elizabeth and Conner were barely on speaking terms. Why would she even *want* to be involved at all? *I shouldn't want to,* Elizabeth realized, ignoring the fact that since she'd frozen in place, she was now blocking traffic and was forcing her fellow students to weave their ways around her. *But I do,* she thought, her heart sinking. Why did she feel so mixed up? Why was she such a mess?

"Liz? You okay?" Evan asked, hesitating as Jade started to walk away.

"Yes. I'm fine," she responded, gripping her tray and taking a step forward.

Elizabeth shook her head. Forget what she'd said earlier. *That* was the understatement of the year. She took another step, glancing around for her friends' table.

Actually, it was the understatement of the century.

To: mcdermott@cal.rr.com
From: alannaf@swiftnet.com
Subject: Where are you?

Conner . . .
   I called you last night. Did you
not get my message? Is everything okay
back at home? At school?
   I have a lot to tell you. And I
really want to see you. I'm starting
to get worried—at least just let me
know everything is all right.
                           Miss you,
                           Alanna

CHAPTER
No Pressure
9

I'm not even hungry, Conner realized as he headed out of class on Tuesday. Still, he figured he might as well go and find his friends in the cafeteria. Normally he preferred to be alone, but ever since the Alanna phone call last night, all Conner wanted was to be distracted from his own thoughts.

She shouldn't be calling me, Conner told himself as he ambled down the long hallway toward the cafeteria. But Conner knew that was stupid. He and Alanna had something together, and she had every right to want to speak to him. It wasn't her fault that he was a mess.

She was just unlucky enough to get involved with me, Conner thought, letting out a sigh. Well, whatever. Conner wasn't going to deal with it now. In fact, he wasn't going to deal with it at all. For the moment Alanna was forgotten. She had to be. Otherwise he was going to lose it.

I'll just chill with everyone and listen to their mindless chatter instead, Conner thought, walking through the cafeteria's entrance. He headed for the food line to grab an orange juice, looking around for his friends' table. But when he finally spotted the crew, sitting at a table against the far wall, his neck muscles stiffened.

Elizabeth was with them.

Without so much as a second thought, Conner immediately strode out, heading back into the hall before Elizabeth glimpsed him. Of course, Conner had known deep down that Elizabeth would be there. Why wouldn't she be? But when he saw her in the flesh, saw her insanely turquoise eyes and gorgeous blond hair, saw her *smile* . . .

He massaged the back of his neck, slumping toward the stairwell. The problem was, every time Conner saw Elizabeth, he was hit by a ton of conflicting thoughts and emotions. Ones that were too overwhelming to get a handle on—how attracted he still was to her, how bad he felt about everything he'd done to her and kept from her, how much he cared about her, how much he cared about *Alanna*, the question of whether he and Alanna would ever work outside of rehab, and the question of whether he and Elizabeth could ever be together again.

Conner's head pounded from all the thoughts that were crammed in there.

He pushed open the door to the stairwell and

started to head up the gray steps. Since Conner didn't think he was going to be able to figure any of this out anytime soon, the best solution would be for him to avoid Elizabeth altogether.

Just like I'm doing with Alanna. Conner adjusted his backpack as he walked, centering it on both shoulders, the weight suddenly feeling very heavy. Too heavy. Yeah. Avoidance was his best route. No question. He'd just stay away from Elizabeth at all costs.

Conner paused on the second-floor landing and kicked at the edge of the wall, squinting at the brilliant afternoon sunshine that was streaming through the small, round window.

There was one glitch with Conner's plan, though. All Conner wanted to do—all he could think about doing—was kissing Elizabeth. Conner rolled his eyes at his own stupidity.

The basic fact was, avoiding Elizabeth seemed highly unlikely.

After lunch on Tuesday, Ken was a man on a mission. And he had absolutely zero qualms about what he was about to do. *I'd hope someone would do the same for me if they saw a way to bring me and Maria back together,* he reasoned as he scanned the bustling postlunch hallway. Will's hobbling figure wasn't hard to spot in the crowd, and Ken's heart went out to the guy as he saw a classmate step off to the side to make a clear passageway for Will to walk through.

Suddenly Ken was brought back to the beginning of the year, when he had been too depressed to play football. But not being on the team had only ended up making things worse. Ken was beyond thankful that with Maria's help, he was able to work his way back onto the field.

Ken shook his head, then headed straight for Will. He knew that he wasn't able to give Will the same gift of playing football again, but if he could make the guy feel a little better about things and bring him back together with an important person in his life, maybe that would help.

"Hey, Simmons," Ken said.

Will glanced over his shoulder. "Hey, Matthews. What's up?"

Ken shook his head. "Not much." He stepped up next to Will. "It's just that the team needs you to do something—and it's kinda short notice."

"Yeah?" Will moved off to the side, leaning all of his weight on one crutch. "What's that?"

"You know how there's that huge pep rally on Friday?" Will nodded. "Well, the captain of the football team is supposed to plan it with the head cheerleader," Ken explained, carefully leaving out the fact that Melissa would be taking Tia's place.

Will stared back at Ken with a blank expression. "Yeah. So? You're the captain now. What's this have to do with me?"

Ken looped his fingers through his khakis' belt loops and made a point of looking Will right in the eye. "I'm *acting* captain, Simmons. You're the team's real captain. We need you to do this."

Will let out a frustrated sigh. "Coach is feeling sorry for me, right? This is a pity gesture, isn't it?"

Ken raised his eyebrows. Will was a harder sell than he'd expected. "Having you plan this wasn't Coach's idea," Ken countered. "It was the team's."

Will's eyes widened. He pulled his body up a little straighter, taking some of his weight off his crutch. "It was?"

Now Ken was getting somewhere. "Yeah. Of course. Actually, at first Coach asked me to do it since you weren't there, but then all the guys came up to me and said they thought that you should be in charge." Ken shrugged, feeling more comfortable now that he was telling Will the almost-whole truth. "Everyone thinks of *you* as captain. Definitely not me." As Will digested this information, Ken added, "I think they'd be really disappointed if you didn't do it. I *know* they'd be."

Will smiled, his features noticeably softening.

"Oh. Well, in that case . . . what do I have to do?"

Ken grinned. *Bingo!* "The meeting's tomorrow night at seven-thirty. House of Java."

"Okay. Sure. I'll be there," Will said, conviction evident in his voice. He leaned his weight back on both crutches and started to move away.

Ken was about to walk away himself when Will paused, shooting Ken a glance. "Matthews," Will called.

Ken paused as well, meeting Will's gaze.

"Thanks," Will said. Then he turned back around and continued on his way.

But Ken lingered there a second longer, basking in the moment. He didn't care what anyone said. With the amazing way he was now feeling, that *had* to be the right thing to do. Ken mentally patted himself on the back as he strolled away.

He could really get into this karma thing.

Did I really think this would be fun? Tia wondered.

It was Tuesday afternoon, and Tia and Andy were squished next to each other on a forest green love seat in the middle of the *Test Your Love* set, minutes away from being taped for a show that was going to be broadcast nationally.

Tia was beyond nervous. Her heart was beating so fast, she could barely keep track of it, even though its loud thumps were sounding in her ears. She hated all the powder that the makeup woman had insisted on applying to her face, plus Tia had made the mistake of wearing a cropped sweater to the taping. The heat from the glaring overhead lights were making her sweat uncontrollably.

I'm going to look like such a fool on TV, Tia thought, swallowing as she watched the studio audience begin to take their seats across from her.

Andy cocked his head, giving Tia a sideways smile. "Check out the competition. We are so gonna smoke them."

Tia leaned forward and glanced at the couple that was sitting on the love seat on the other side of Andy. They were both very jocky looking, the girl with a bouncing blond ponytail and red Converse sneakers, the guy with a bulky frame and an almost crew cut. They seemed harmless enough, but then again, they were also a real couple. Which meant that they had a leg up on Tia and Andy.

At that thought the butterflies in Tia's stomach intensified. Trying to ignore the flutters, Tia turned her head and looked the other way, at the couple sitting on the love seat to her left. And her jaw dropped open. They were making out! Right there—in front of everyone! Some of the members of the audience began to whistle and cheer, and a

PA, looking embarrassed, quickly hurried over and asked the couple to cool it down. Pulling away from her long-haired boyfriend, the girl flipped her dark hair over her shoulder and giggled, which only caused the audience to cheer more.

Now Tia was in full-out panic mode. She was sweating so much, she wished she could just rip off her clothes. *That* would make the audience cheer.

"What makes you think we can beat *them?*" Tia asked, turning back to Andy.

Andy shrugged, stretching his legs out in front of him. "Because we're the smoothest around," he joked. "It's in the cards."

"Andy, I'm serious," Tia said, widening her eyes. "Those people are really going out. We're not. We're going to look like idiots!"

"No, no, you're wrong there." Andy sat forward, dropping his voice to the quietest whisper. "See, it works against them that they're really together."

Tia wiped her sweaty palms against her black cotton pants. "How do you figure *that?*"

"Because they have more at stake. If they tank out here, they could end up fighting and then breaking up. That means they have to be feeling a lot more pressure—which translates into them being a lot more nervous . . . which means they have a greater likelihood of messing up."

127

Tia blinked at Andy's little analysis, impressed . . . and somewhat calmed. "You've really thought this through, haven't you?"

Andy grinned. He leaned back into the love seat again, folding his arms behind his neck. "Yes. Yes, I *really* want to win that trip to New York."

Tia took in the relaxed manner in which Andy was sitting and the confident demeanor on his face. She shook her head, amazed. "Aren't you even the least bit nervous?"

Andy appeared to consider this for a moment, then abruptly shook his head. "Nah. Not really."

Tia simply couldn't understand it. They were going to start filming any second, and Andy looked so calm, he could have been sitting on his couch at home. It was so annoying! "Why not?" she demanded. "We're going to be on TV!"

Andy sat forward, placing both of his hands on Tia's narrow shoulders. "You must chill out," he told her. "Seriously. Think about it this way—the producers chose us because they thought we were good—great, actually. Better than the hundreds of other couples that showed up. Right?"

Tia chewed on the inside of her lip as she considered this. "I guess. . . ."

"So? They know what they're doing. We're going to rock," Andy assured her.

Tia glanced down at her gold bangle bracelet, twisting it around her wrist. Andy *did* have a point. They had kicked butt in all of the auditions. Of course, there'd been no live audience or complete camera crews around, but Tia would just have to ignore them now. She drew in a deep breath and closed her eyes, feeling her heartbeat slow down as she did so. *You're going to be fine,* she told herself.

"Hey, guys. Just wanted to wish you good luck."

Tia opened her eyes to see Matt crouching before her and Andy, looking as hot as ever in a blue T-shirt and jeans. Her heart sped up again—but this time it wasn't out of nervousness.

"Thanks," she said, flashing Matt a smile.

"No problem." Matt stood up and winked, an adorable dimple popping out on his left cheek. "You know what?" he whispered. "You guys are gonna win. I can feel it." Then he jogged off, running over to the producer who had called his name.

Still smiling, Tia grasped the edge of the chair's cushion. *That* was all she needed—a little encouragement from the sexiest guy in California. If he was rooting for them . . . well, Tia was quickly becoming a believer.

Finally relaxing, Tia scooted back into the love seat, crossing one leg over the other. She could think about it this way—if for some reason she and Andy *didn't* win, Tia would then be free to ask Matt out.

And in that case, losing wouldn't exactly be the worst thing.

Andy simply couldn't believe it. Kip Carson looked even more plastic in person than he did on TV. The game-show host had just strode onto the set, taking his seat in the armchair at the far left, and Andy couldn't help marveling at how stiff the guy's blond hair appeared to be. It looked like not even a tractor would be capable of moving his locks. Not to mention Kip's "tanned" skin—the dude was practically orange!

It was comforting for Andy to focus on Kip's absurd physical details. That way he could ignore the fact that he was nervous. Okay, so Andy had told Tia that he was perfectly calm. Which he had been up until a moment ago. But now that Kip was onstage and the crew had quieted down the studio audience *and* they were seconds away from starting, Andy was beginning to feel those anxious vibes swimming in his stomach.

"Hey," Tia whispered, giving Andy a pinch on his arm. "It's almost time. Good luck."

"Um, yeah, you too," Andy responded, looking back at Tia in amazement. The girl was smiling and appeared to be totally relaxed while Andy was in the middle of an internal freak-out session. And he had been the one to calm Tia down in the first place!

Andy scratched his head as he looked out at the studio audience. *What did I say to her again?* He crossed one leg over the other and then uncrossed it, deciding to look down at the checkerboard tiled floor instead of at the people watching him. *Oh, yeah, yeah. That they must've chosen us for a reason. That we're gonna rock. We've come this far, after all.*

Andy felt his pulse start to slow down as he reminded himself of his words of wisdom. Unfortunately, though, Andy's pep talk was cut short when all of the lights on the set were suddenly switched off. Then a balding man with a huge belly hanging over his jeans, who was standing in between the audience and the set, bellowed out a countdown.

"Three, two, one . . . ," the guy called, then pointed right at the stage.

Before Andy could even process what was happening, the bright lights were flipped back on, *Test Your Love*'s horrible theme song was playing, and the audience was cheering and clapping. Andy was definitely sweating, but he almost didn't have time to be nervous. It was all happening so fast.

Tia gave Andy's arm another pinch as Kip said his hellos and gave a brief explanation of the very simple rules of the game show. And then, before

Andy knew it, they were already on the first question.

Andy blinked. This was so surreal. Kip Carson was actually leaning forward in his armchair, looking at Andy and the two other "boyfriends" with mock interest after asking them in a baritone voice, "What activity does your girlfriend love to do that you find completely boring?"

Andy felt frozen in place. All he could do was stare like an idiot as Kip looked at all the girls and added, "Remember, ladies. You have to guess what your boyfriend's response is going to be."

Andy's mouth dropped open. Now he had to actually answer this question! On national television. Andy and Tia had never even discussed this topic in their practice sessions. How were they supposed to get this right?

Andy clasped his clammy hands, fidgeting with his fingers as he glanced at Tia. She didn't appear to be conflicted at all. She was very calmly typing her answer into her little red computer thing—the one that looked like a handheld organizer and would then display her answer on the TV screen when it was their turn to respond. Somehow Tia seemed confident in predicting what Andy was going to say.

But I don't even know what I'm going to say, Andy thought, licking his lips. He looked down at his watch. *How much time do they give us anyway?*

A bell-like ding sound rang out. Andy stiffened. *Great. That's it. Time's up.* Andy panicked, wringing his hands. *Quick. Think. What's Tee like to do that bores me?* It was as if the cameras and bright lights were stripping Andy's mind of any thoughts whatsoever.

"All righty," Kip said, flashing the couples a smile to reveal his overly white teeth. "Let's see if you guys are all grooving on the same wavelength."

Andy winced, receiving a break from his panic as he observed how ridiculous Kip sounded when he tried to use "young-and-hip" lingo.

Kip turned his attention to couple number one. "So. Danny." Kip glanced down at the red index card he was holding in the palm of his hand. "What does Jenna like to do that you think is a total drag?"

Danny moved to the edge of his seat. "Okay. Yeah." He nodded, his dark eyes lighting up as he gave a devilish grin. "I've got it." Danny paused dramatically for a moment, rolling his shoulders forward and back. "Okay, hanging out with her family. Totally boring." As Danny said the words, he actually looked pleased with himself.

Jenna, on the other hand, was anything but pleased. She let out a little gasp, then slapped Danny on his bulky shoulder.

133

Andy laughed, completely forgetting about his anxiety for the moment. *What an idiot,* he thought, shaking his head. It was as if the dude forgot that millions of people—including Jenna's family—would be watching this. And then Andy realized something—he'd been right. This *was* going to be easier for him and Tia since they had nothing at stake. *No pressure,* Andy reminded himself, settling into the love seat so that he was comfortable. *Just relax. Be cool.*

"Yikes," Kip said, his eyes twinkling. "Hope you're not planning on going over to Jenna's for dinner anytime soon." The audience laughed, and Kip shook his head. "Nope. I'm afraid Jenna's answer was 'shopping.'"

Jenna slapped Danny one more time. "Ow!" he yelped.

Kip held out a hand as if he were stopping traffic. "Easy. You're only on the first question, guys." Then Kip looked at Andy. "Let's see if you fared any better. What's your answer on this one, Andy?"

Oh, man. Andy's heart started beating in his ears. He couldn't believe it was his turn already. He had finally come up with a response, but he was still worried about sounding like an idiot. Andy swallowed. *Whatever. Here goes.*

He sat forward in the chair. "Well, uh, Kip, the

thing is, Tia really loves watching baseball—and football—on TV . . . and I don't." Andy clasped his hands, the words sounding stupid as soon as he heard them come out of his mouth.

"So, that's your answer?" Kip asked, staring right at Andy. "Watching sports?"

Andy's neck started to heat up. *That's so the wrong answer,* he thought, his mouth drying up. "Yeah."

Andy was just waiting for Tia to whack him for his stupidity when he heard her exclaim, *"Yes!"*

"Good work! Your responses matched," Kip announced.

Relief washing over him, Andy turned to Tia, who was beaming. He held out his hand as she reached out to slap him five. "We *rock,*" she said, her dark eyes sparkling.

Kip turned to the audience. "I don't know about you guys, but I'm just glad we didn't have another fight on our hands."

When Andy found himself laughing along at Kip's lame joke, he realized that he was now going to be in fine shape for the rest of the show. He could handle this. Andy grinned, stretching his arms above his head. Plus he was sure that he and Tia had a really good shot at winning.

And Andy turned out to be right. He and Tia ended up matching on almost every response. The

135

only thing that Andy hadn't predicted was just how quickly the whole thing would go. Before he knew it, he and Tia were battling it out with couple number three in the lightning round (Danny and Jenna had barely scored the entire time). Whoever won this final round would win the game. And, more important in Andy's mind, the trip to New York.

But Andy wasn't thinking about that now. All he could manage to do was spew out the one-word answers to the questions thrown at him, trying to get as many out as possible in the time allotted.

"Finesse!" he screamed in response to Kip's question, "Favorite shampoo?" Andy was sweating like crazy with his hands balled into fists, ready to yell out the next answer, when the bell sounded.

Andy let out a sigh of relief, relaxing his shoulders and his hands. He didn't think he could go on much longer. But he also didn't know if they'd won. It was impossible to keep track of how many right answers all of them had gotten.

"Okay, here's how it goes down," Kip began. "Juan and Julia, you two got a combined total of fifteen correct responses in the lightning round. Andy and Tia, your total comes to . . . seventeen—you win!"

Andy jumped up immediately, pulling Tia into a hug as she sprang up as well.

"We won, we won!" she exclaimed, hopping up and down.

"Whoo-hoo!" Andy yelled. "We're going to New York!"

The cheesy theme music started to play as Kip strolled over to congratulate Andy and Tia. And then, without even fully realizing what he was doing, Andy began to do a victory dance with Kip and Tia—something he knew for certain that he'd regret later.

But who cared? They won! He was going to New York!

The bald crew guy made a slashing movement across his neck with his hand, indicating that they were done taping. The theme music started to fade out, and Kip was off the stage and into the dressing room in almost two seconds flat. But Andy was still dancing.

"I can't believe we're going to New York!" he said to Tia.

She laughed. "I know! How cool is that?"

The crew guys were starting to clear out the set, and Matt walked over, patting both Andy and Tia on the back. "Good work, guys. Told you you'd win," he said, grinning.

"Yo, Matt!" a curly-haired PA called from across the set. "Stop flirting and get your butt over here!"

Matt gave Andy and Tia a sheepish look and

shrugged. "Whoops. What can I say? Guess I'm needed." He smiled one more time, then headed off to help out the PA.

Tia's mouth dropped so wide open, her bottom lip almost touched the floor. "Did you hear that?" she asked excitedly, grasping Andy's arm. "That guy said Matt was *flirting!*"

Andy looked at Tia in disbelief. How could she even begin to care about that when they'd just found out that they won? That they were going to New York? "So?"

Tia widened her dark brown eyes. "*So,* that means he really is flirting, which means he really likes me. Which means I have to ask him out. Now." Tia headed straight for Matt.

But Andy grabbed her arm and pulled her back toward him, convinced she was losing her mind. "You're supposed to be my girlfriend, remember?" he said. "Do you want to get disqualified from the show?"

Tia blinked. "Oh. Right." She frowned, chewing on the inside of her lip. Then she looked down at the floor, suddenly sullen.

Andy rolled his eyes. How could Tia be ruining this exciting moment just because she couldn't ask a guy out? *It's not like she won't have a million other opportunities,* Andy thought. *Unlike me.*

"Wait a minute. I know!" Tia glanced back up, her face brightened. "How about if I just tell him the truth but beg him to keep our secret? He probably would, right?"

Andy rolled his eyes. "Right. I'm sure he'd risk losing his job just so that we wouldn't get found out." Tia's smile disappeared, and Andy added, "C'mon, Tee. Can't you just hold off until after we go to New York? It would suck to have gotten this far only to get thrown out."

Tia sighed but nodded. "Yeah. I guess you're right." She took a moment to shoot a dramatic longing look in Matt's direction. "He can wait . . . I hope." But when Tia turned back to Andy, she was all smiles. "Well? Let's go tell everyone we won!"

Andy smiled back at her, relieved. There was the Tia he knew and loved.

To: jaames@cal.rr.com
From: jess1@cal.rr.com
Subject: Crazy

Hi, there! How was your day? Did your history test go okay? As if I even need to ask, Mr. History Whiz.

Everyone around me is acting totally crazy. Liz is completely bugged out because Conner is home, and she's been in a funk. Tia has been pretending that Andy is her boyfriend just to get on *Test Your Love*. And Jade actually gushed to me the other day about Evan. She's like a different person.

What would you say if I told you that I'm the only normal person around?

To: jess1@cal.rr.com
From: jaames@cal.rr.com
Subject: re: Crazy

I'd be scared. Very scared.

CHAPTER 10
There's This Girl

"Your boss wasn't mad that you're taking a break, was she?" Maria asked Elizabeth that afternoon as the two of them headed out of Sedona together.

Elizabeth let out a frustrated sigh. "Maybe, but that's her problem. I needed it."

As usual, Elizabeth's job, complete with demanding customers, an unpleasant boss, and headache-inducing perfume smells, was totally stressing her out.

They passed a paper-and-card store, its window display filled with party items—happy-birthday banners, balloons, brightly colored ribbons, and noisemakers. Maria turned to Elizabeth, pushing one of her dark curls behind her ear. "Are you going to Conner's party tomorrow?"

Elizabeth's stomach turned over. Tia had told Elizabeth about the party at lunch. And Elizabeth's brain had been consumed over the dilemma over whether or not she should go ever since then. *Forget*

141

the job, she thought, biting her lip. *This whole Conner thing is why I'm such a mess.*

Maria winced, obviously reading Elizabeth's expression. "Oops. Sorry. Bad subject?"

"No." Elizabeth moved aside so that a woman pushing a double-seated stroller could get by. "I mean, yes." She shook her head, giving Maria a sad smile. "I'm totally pathetic, aren't I?"

"Why? Because you're confused? Considering what you guys have been through, I think that's completely normal." At that moment a group of pre-teen boys dressed in skater clothes rushed by, knocking the strap of Maria's dark green purse off her shoulder. "Hey! Watch it!" Maria called after the kids, pulling her bag up off the shiny mall floor.

A gray-haired woman with a cane momentarily stopped walking to pat Maria's arm. "You tell them," she said, then continued to shuffle off.

Elizabeth laughed. "I'm glad you stopped by. I needed a distraction. You know what? Let's not talk about Conner or the party anymore. It only brings me down."

"Okay, fine." Maria nodded, now firmly holding on to her purse. But as they reached Stereo City, the electronics store where Maria had wanted to go to look for a Discman, she paused, her brow furrowing. "Can I just give you my input, though? Then I swear I'll drop the subject."

142

"Sure," Elizabeth responded, moving away from the store's entrance so that they weren't blocking traffic. "Go ahead. It can't possibly make me more confused."

"All right," Maria said, watching Elizabeth with a careful expression. "I think you should go."

"You do?" Elizabeth asked. She was about to launch into the many reasons why she thought she *shouldn't* go, but Maria spoke before she did.

"Just listen for a sec," Maria said, holding up a hand. "It won't mean that you want to get back together with the guy or anything. It'll just mean that you support him. Which you do, right? I mean, you are glad he went through rehab. And you probably want him to stick with it, don't you?"

"Well, yes," Elizabeth said, fidgeting with her silver-heart necklace. "But . . ." Her voice trailed off, her thoughts too jumbled for her to try to make any sense of them.

Maria shrugged. "That's just my two cents. You still need to figure out what *you* think you should do." Maria headed back over to Stereo City's entrance, pulling Elizabeth along with her. "Oo-kay. That's enough heaviness for now. Go distract yourself with all of the high-tech goodies."

Elizabeth followed Maria through the store's open doors, but she knew that she was beyond distraction. *Am I going to be confused forever?* she wondered.

Maria stopped in front of one of the enormous

big-screen TVs, shaking her head as she watched Laura Linsley, a raven-haired actress on the soap opera *Always Tomorrow*, overact a monologue.

"I just don't know what to do," the actress sobbed. She grasped the edges of her desk, her blue eyes rolling heavenward. "Please. Someone. Tell me what to do!"

Maria laughed. "It should be illegal to be that huge of a drama queen," she commented, then continued to head toward the portable-stereo section.

But Elizabeth remained rooted in front of the TV, her stomach dropping.

"I'm so *confused*," Laura Linsley wailed on the thirty-six-inch screen.

Oh my God, Elizabeth thought, transfixed by the television. *I'm becoming a drama queen.*

That was it. *I have to make a decision about Conner and move on with my life,* she resolved, walking over to where Maria was examining a Discman. *I can't stay confused forever.*

And her first step would be to make a firm decision about tomorrow's party. *I'm going to go. Period. Final decision.* Elizabeth stepped up next to Maria, feeling a little queasy.

Unless, of course, I change my mind . . .

Andy was still flying high a little while later, visions of New York City floating through his head.

He and Tia were backstage, where one of the crew members had given them all of this paperwork to sign and had then explained that they would be getting their plane tickets and other information in a few days. But Andy had barely focused on a word the guy had said. He'd been too busy figuring out all the places he wanted to see in Manhattan.

Times Square, SoHo, Greenwich Village, the twin towers . . .

It was almost time to go home, and Andy was still busy planning, imagining how cool this whole trip was going to be, as he leaned against the cool concrete wall, his arms crossed over his chest, waiting for Tia to come back from the bathroom.

"Hey. Congrats again," said Matt, the way-too-cute crew guy, walking over.

Andy stared back at Matt and wondered what on earth he was doing being a PA, running errands for all of the higher-ups. *He could be an actor. Or a model,* Andy thought, taking in Matt's rugged good looks.

"Thanks," Andy responded.

Matt glanced from the left to the right, his hazel eyes searching. Then he looked back at Andy. "Where's Tia?"

"Bathroom," Andy said, suddenly thinking he possibly had been a little overly harsh with Tia on this whole Matt thing. Clearly the guy *was* interested. . . .

Matt rocked back on his heels, an earnest expression falling over his chiseled features. "Yeah, well, listen. I'm sorry about that flirting comment—if it made you uncomfortable, I mean."

Andy blinked, pulling up the sleeves of his rugby shirt. "What? Oh, no. It's fine." *Now* Andy was uncomfortable, though. He really didn't want Matt to apologize for hitting on his "girlfriend." It would make him feel like an even bigger creep for lying. "Don't worry about it."

"Glad you feel that way." Half of Matt's mouth drew up into a lopsided smile, his deep-set eyes sparkling. "Can't help it if I think it's a shame you have a girlfriend. We could've hung out, you know?"

What? All Andy could do was stand there like an idiot, paralyzed by the wave of disbelief that washed over him. *Is he saying what I think he's saying? Is he flirting with* me?

"Let me know if you guys break up." Matt winked and patted Andy on his shoulder, then strolled away, leaving Andy to stand there with his mouth hanging open.

Oh my God. He was flirting, Andy realized, nerves shooting across his stomach. The hot crew guy was flirting with me. Then Andy broke out into a smile. Cool. He felt like laughing. In fact, he did start laughing.

"Andy? You okay?"

Andy looked to his left to see Tia stepping up next to him, her hands on her hips.

"I mean, I know you're excited about going to New York and all, but—"

"Tee, you're not going to believe what just happened," Andy broke in. When Tia closed her mouth Andy added, "It's about Matt."

Tia's entire face lit up as if she was a little girl about to open a Christmas gift. "Oh my God. What did he say? Was it about me?"

"Nope." Andy drew in a sharp breath, feeling mighty pleased with himself. "It was about *me*."

Tiny lines of confusion broke out across Tia's wide forehead. "Huh? What do you mean?"

Andy threw his hands in the air. "What I mean is, Matt made it very clear that all this time he's been hitting on *me*. I'm the one he's interested in."

Tia blinked, her eyes widening into enormous circles. "Shut up. You're not serious."

"I'm totally serious. Trust me. I wouldn't make this kind of thing up."

Tia brought a hand up to her mouth, the evidence of a smile starting to show. "You mean he's gay?"

Andy nodded. "Apparently."

Tia shook her head and brought her hand away from her mouth, her smile now out in full force. "Of course. Someone that perfect would have to be gay."

Andy dropped his hands into his corduroy pants'

front pockets. "Yeah. That's what they say about me," he joked.

"Oh God. You're not going to get all cocky on me now, are you?" Tia asked, playfully hitting Andy's arm.

"Nah. I'll keep my thoughts of studliness to myself."

"Very funny," Tia said. She linked her arm through Andy's, starting to walk with him to the door that led to the parking garage. But then she stopped in place. "Wait a minute. I hope you know that the same rules apply to you."

"What rules?"

Tia looked around to see if anyone was close by, then dropped her voice to a whisper. "The rule that says you can't ask Matt out. Otherwise we might get caught."

Andy shrugged and continued to walk. Asking Matt out hadn't even crossed his mind. He was just flattered that a guy like him would be interested. "Yeah. Okay. Fine."

The two friends reached the door, and Tia pulled it open. "Man," she said, walking ahead of Andy to the stairwell. "If *your* social life starts to become more exciting than mine, I'm going to just die."

Andy laughed, watching Tia's tiny figure retreat down the stairs. "Hey, thanks," he called after her. "Way to bring a guy down."

But the truth was, nothing was going to bring Andy down tonight. He whistled to himself, happily jogging down the stairs, taking them two at a time. *What a day.* Andy had been taped for a TV show, won a trip to New York, and been hit on by a very cute guy.

And my life is now anything but boring.

Jade, Elizabeth, rehab . . .

Evan sat at a small, round table by the front window at House of Java, munching on a mocha-chip cookie and mentally listing the conversation topics he wanted to avoid when Conner came back from the bathroom.

It was weird. Conner was one of Evan's best friends, and he couldn't be more psyched to have him back home. But because of everything that had gone on the past few weeks, there were now all of these off-limits subjects between them, which made Evan very uncomfortable.

Take Jade, for example. Things were going so well with her, and Evan had been more than happy that she'd made it to his swim meet after school today. The girl was basically always on his mind. But Evan didn't really want to talk about her with Conner because yapping about girls could lead to the mention of Elizabeth. Seeing as *that* topic made Evan feel majorly guilty, it was another one to avoid. And Conner himself had made it very clear that he didn't want to discuss rehab at all.

So what do *we talk about?* Evan wondered, gulping down a sip of his iced coffee. *The weather?*

"Your stroke's looking nice, man," Conner remarked as he sat down in the chair across from Evan.

Swimming. That was a harmless topic. "Thanks," Evan responded, grabbing up the last crumbs of his cookie. "Coach says I might get a scholarship."

"You should." Conner lifted up his mug and took a sip of coffee. "You punished the competition today."

Evan pushed his hair away from his face and smiled. "Don't know about that. But I'll take the compliment."

"Yeah, well, Jade Wu seems to like your swimming style," Conner commented. He leaned back in his wooden seat. "You've been seeing her for a while?"

Evan shrugged. "Not so long," he responded, trying to downplay the whole thing. "She's cool, though." He pressed his lips together. "What about you? Been writing much music?"

Conner lifted his eyebrows. "Yeah. A little." He shifted in his seat, moving his gaze down to his coffee mug. "One song's not bad." Conner was staring at the cup as if it held the answers to life. He grasped its square handle. "It's about Liz."

Evan blinked, stunned that Conner would admit he'd written a song about Elizabeth. The guy was usually completely tight-lipped when it came to emotions or relationships. This was a first. Clearly Conner *wanted* to talk about Elizabeth.

You'd be a bad friend if you changed the subject on him again, Evan thought. He swallowed. *That is, even worse than the one you already are.*

"You thought about her while you were away, huh?" Evan asked, not looking Conner quite in the eye.

Conner finally glanced up from the mug. "I guess." He ran his fingers along the rounded edge of the black table. "Not that it matters."

"What do you mean?" Evan realized he was delving into dangerous territory, risking having all of his Elizabeth guilt rise to the surface by asking this question, but he didn't care. His friendship with Conner was more important than his own discomfort.

"I mean that I . . . want her back," Conner said gruffly. He sat forward, looking down at his hands. "But it's not gonna happen."

Did Evan say he didn't mind the discomfort? Because at the moment he was seriously regretting going down this path. Evan's stomach twisted, but there was no turning back now. "Why not?"

Conner glanced up again. This time it felt like his eyes were searing right into Evan's. "Some things are standing in the way," he said with a shrug.

Oh, man. Evan felt nerves shoot up and down his arms. What was Conner getting at? Did he know about

151

Evan and Elizabeth? *Maybe this whole conversation is a trap,* Evan thought, beyond paranoid. *Maybe he's going to lash out at me any second for betraying him.*

Evan licked his lips. "Um, like what?" Man, was he dreading Conner's answer.

Conner rolled his eyes upward, then shook his head. He looked like he was annoyed at Evan for asking the question.

Evan cringed inwardly. He grabbed the soft edges of his brown leather seat cushion. *Here it comes. . . .*

Conner let out a sigh. "There's this girl."

Evan blinked. His grip on the seat cushion loosened. "Wait a minute. A girl? What girl?" he asked, relieved and confused at the same time.

"Alanna," Conner said, color tinging his angular cheeks. "We hooked up in rehab."

"She was there for counseling too?" Evan's brain was reeling. "Isn't that sort of against the rules, Conner?"

"Yeah." Conner downed the last sips of his coffee, then pushed the mug away from him. "But it happened." He grabbed a napkin and wiped off his mouth. "She's cool. She's from around here."

"Huh," Evan said, sitting forward. "So what are you going to do? I mean, are you guys, like, still together?"

"Don't know." Conner picked up one of the white sugar packets out of the little black holder in the center of the table and turned it over and over in his hands. "I'm still into her. But I'm also still into Liz." Conner tossed the sugar packet aside. "And I don't think Liz would be psyched to hear that I met someone."

Evan stared back at his friend, almost at a loss for words. The thing was, there was so much he could say. For one, Evan could tell Conner that Elizabeth had hooked up while he was gone too. That he hadn't been the only one to meet someone else. *But you promised Liz you'd let her be the one to tell Conner about us,* Evan reminded himself.

Then again, Evan wasn't sure if his loyalties should lie with her. If they did, then shouldn't he tell Elizabeth about this Alanna girl?

Sitting across from Conner, Evan realized that would be a bad move. *I've already betrayed him once as it is,* Evan thought, his cheeks heating up. *I'm not going to do it again.*

Feeling slightly queasy about the whole ugly situation, Evan decided to just stay out of it and let Conner and Elizabeth be the ones to straighten everything out. It was their relationship, after all.

"That's tough," Evan said, finally speaking up. "But you'll figure it out."

At least, Evan hoped Conner would. Because he sure couldn't.

*   *   *

153

Ken didn't know why, but he always felt better about things when he was driving. The slightly mindless activity of steering the wheel and following the lines of the road usually helped to clear his mind. And man, did his mind need clearing tonight.

Ken sighed, putting on his turn signal before making a left onto Palm Drive. He just couldn't get Maria out of his brain. He kept replaying and replaying the conversation that he'd had with her today—she'd seemed like she was warming up to him. But then, what did that mean? That he had a shot of getting back together with her? Or just that Maria was beginning to think that he wasn't a *total* jerk and that maybe they could be friends again one day?

Ken dropped his head to the steering wheel for a moment as he waited at a red light. He didn't know what Maria was thinking. All he knew was that she had not looked happy when Melissa had strolled over and interrupted their conversation. *Not happy at all.* Ken lifted his head, pressing on the gas pedal as the traffic light turned green. His heart sank as he realized that because of the little maneuver that Melissa had pulled today, he might be back at square one with Maria.

And you probably deserve it, Ken told himself, gripping the wheel more tightly. Spotting the lighted black-and-white sign for House of Java up on his right, Ken decided that he'd drop in and grab a cup of coffee. He could continue driving around, but his thoughts were beginning to make him crazy. And odds were that someone Ken knew would be inside. Distracting himself and taking his mind off Maria for a little while definitely couldn't hurt.

It's worth a try anyway, Ken thought, pulling into House of Java's crowded parking lot. Finding a space next to the garbage bins, he parked, then jumped out and headed over to the coffee shop's front entrance.

And as soon as he walked through the clear glass doors, the scent of ground coffee beans assaulting his nose, Ken saw that he'd predicted right. Conner, Evan, Andy, and Tia were all sitting at a corner table over by the window, laughing at something. Ken wasn't exactly close with any of them, but he was sure they could distract him for a little while, at least.

"Hey, Matthews," Andy called, spotting him. "What's up?"

Ken walked over to the four friends, running a hand through his blond hair. "Not much. Just needed to get out of the house."

"Well, pop a squat." Andy motioned to the empty chair in between Conner and Tia. "Join us in our victory party."

"Victory party?" Ken repeated as he dropped down into the brown, vintage-looking armchair. "For what?"

Evan, who was sitting on the other side of Tia, rolled his eyes. "Don't ask."

"Oh, come on," Tia chided. "You're just jealous."

Evan laughed. "Oh, yeah. You're right. I've always wanted to be on *Test Your Love* with my fake girl-friend."

"What's he talking about?" Ken asked, totally confused. Still, he grinned. These four were good for a distraction, no question about that.

"Tee and I pretended to be a couple and went on *Test Your Love,*" Andy explained. He took a sip from a jumbo-sized cup of hot chocolate, then wiggled his red-blond eyebrows. "And we *won.*"

Ken blinked, letting out a chuckle. "Really?"

"Yes!" Tia beamed. She was practically bouncing up and down in her straight-back seat. "*And* our prize is a trip to New York."

Ken glanced from Tia to Andy. He was having a hard time buying this out-there story. But they both looked completely psyched. And besides, who could make up something like that? "Wow," Ken said, sitting back and crossing his arms over his chest. "That's pretty cool."

"Thank you," Tia said. She turned to Evan, shooting him a mock glare. "See? Some people are happy for us."

"Hey, if you feel okay about *lying* on national

television, who am I to stop you?" Evan joked, shrugging.

Andy let out a dramatic sigh. "*Please.* As if TV is all about reality."

As Evan and Andy continued on with their debate, Ken turned uncomfortably to Conner. Ken hadn't uttered a word to the guy in school the past couple of days. They weren't exactly best friends before Conner had left for rehab, and now Ken really wasn't sure what the right thing was to say. It wasn't as if Hallmark made appropriate cards for the occasion or anything.

Should I just ignore the whole thing? Ken wondered. *Not even bring it up?* But then, that seemed idiotic. Conner had been gone for weeks.

"So," Ken said to Conner, pulling at the frayed edge of his flannel shirt. "How have things, you know, how have they been?"

Conner's green eyes darkened. "Fine," he responded. He crumpled up his napkin into a ball.

Ken fidgeted with his hands as he realized that he'd opted for the wrong approach. *Not bringing it up definitely would have been the right way to go.*

"What about you?" Conner asked after a long, quiet moment. "Did you and Maria break up or something?"

Ken's face heated up. He was taken aback by the

bluntness of Conner's question. *So much for taking my mind off Maria.*

"Yeah," Ken muttered, looking down at his hands. "We did."

Ken glanced back up, but Conner had turned his head to say something to Andy. Tia shot Ken a look of sympathy, though, her dark eyes wide.

"Hey. You wanna know something?" she asked Ken in a soft voice as she leaned in closer.

Ken kicked at the floor. "What?"

"I think Maria misses you too."

In an instant Ken's heart jumped. He sat up straight. "She does?"

Tia smiled sweetly and nodded. "Of course."

Ken could have kissed the girl. That was, without a doubt, the coolest thing that anyone had said to him in a long time.

And it was all he needed to hear. He was going to get Maria back—whatever it took. They belonged together. Period.

And now that Tia had passed along this information . . . Ken grinned to himself, his hopes lifting and his body suddenly feeling light. If Maria missed him, obviously she wanted him back. Which meant that getting back together with her wasn't even going to be as hard as Ken had feared it would be.

Ken stood, deciding to go get himself a cup of coffee.

"Anyone want anything?" he asked the crew. When they all responded no, Ken strolled over to the counter just the same, checking out all of the oversized muffins and cookies behind the glass counter. He was going to get something supersized for himself.

Because suddenly *he* was in the mood for a victory party.

melissa Fox

To do at the pep-rally meeting:

- Pick an emcee.
- Choose cheers—which ones?
- Decide on costumes.
- Talk about dance sequence—
  maybe have football-team
  dance?
- Discuss music.
- Figure out timing/schedule.
- make sure Ken sees what he's
  missing.

Maria Slater

Poor Liz. This whole Conner thing has her so messed up. And I wish I could help her. But she really needs to decide for herself whether or not she wants him back.

I can sort of relate, though. I mean, I still care about Ken. Obviously I've thought about what it would be like to get back together with him.

But I have it easier than Liz. Because even though I miss Ken at times, I can't forgive him for breaking my heart.

So I'm not confused at all.

CHAPTER

Old Habits

11

I'm just going to get this over with, Melissa told herself, taking a deep breath.

It was Wednesday evening, and she was sitting at a back table at House of Java, waiting for Ken to show up so that they could get this whole pep-rally-planning thing over with. Of course, Melissa wanted to do a good job, but she didn't need Ken's help for that. She would simply listen to whatever the jerk had to say, jot it all down on her yellow legal pad, and then type up what she wanted to propose anyway. She was sure that Ken didn't know the first thing about planning a major event. Meeting him here was just a formality.

Melissa took a sip of her skim latte, glancing down at the watch that hung loosely off her left wrist. Ken was already six minutes late. If he kept her waiting much longer, she was really going to explode on him when he showed up.

Melissa was staring at the front door, thinking about how rude and thoughtless it was to be late, when she suddenly saw Will walk through with his crutches. For a moment Melissa completely lost her train of thought as she took in how well Will's deep blue button-down shirt set off his gray-blue eyes, how perfectly that shirt fit his toned upper body. . . .

Don't even look at him, Melissa thought, her cheeks heating up. *He's not worth your time.* Still, for some reason, Melissa couldn't take her gaze off her ex-boyfriend. It was almost as if she enjoyed the torture.

Until Will took a couple of steps inside and spotted *her,* clearly noticing Melissa looking at him. Melissa quickly glanced away, focusing on the blank pad of paper in front of her instead, but she was too late. Will's face hardened immediately, and he definitely knew that she'd been watching him.

Well, whatever, Melissa thought, picking up her shiny silver pen. *I won't give Will the satisfaction of looking at him again.* She began to write, carefully printing *Pep Rally Ideas* in clean, neat letters on the top of the page. That took all of thirty seconds. Then Melissa stared down at her coffee cup, swirling the foamy milk around with her little metal spoon.

"Have you seen Tia anywhere?"

Melissa's heart almost stopped at the sound of Will's deep voice. Still holding on to the spoon, she slowly looked up at him. His eyes were cold, and his mouth was set in a firm, straight line. Clearly he didn't want to be talking to her. He just wanted information.

Let him find Tia on his own, then, Melissa thought, grasping the spoon more tightly. She was about to glance away and just ignore him completely, but she couldn't help being curious. *Why's he looking for Tia anyway?* she wondered. Her slender shoulders tensed up. If he was going after *Tia,* if he was doing this to make Melissa jealous . . .

"Don't you know? She's throwing some party for Conner tonight," Melissa responded, trying hard to make her voice sound tight and unforgiving. Normally she wouldn't have Tia's calendar memorized or anything, but she'd overheard Tia talking about the party in school earlier.

"*What?*" Will narrowed his eyes, shaking his head in disbelief. He glanced down at his watch. "I was supposed to meet her, like, over ten minutes ago."

"Why?" Melissa blurted out, unable to hide her interest. "What for?"

Will still looked completely baffled. He glanced around the busy coffee shop, as if he was hoping Melissa was wrong and he'd see Tia walk inside any minute. "We were supposed to plan the pep rally."

"The pep rally?" Melissa repeated. "No, you're not. Ken and I were assigned to do that."

Will's gaze went right to Melissa, his eyes piercing hers. "*You* and Ken?" He glanced down at the table, noticing Melissa's legal pad. Slowly he looked back up at her. "Matthews is a dead man."

"What? What are you talking about?" Melissa demanded.

"Ken passed the buck on to me," Will snapped, his eyes flashing. "But if he thinks I'm gonna plan this thing with *you*—" Will broke off for a moment, his entire face turning red. "He's an idiot."

Melissa's lips parted as she processed this information. But then she snapped her mouth shut and clenched her jaw, anger rising inside her. She didn't know what made her more mad—the fact that Ken was going to such lengths to get her and Will back together—obviously just so that he could feel better about himself—or Will's disgusted reaction at having to work with her.

"This is a freakin' nightmare," Will said through his teeth.

Okay. Yeah. Will's reaction.

"Look, I'm not exactly happy about this either," she said. She hated the whiny edge she could hear in her voice. "You're the last person I want to do this with."

"Well, fine. Perfect," Will responded shortly. "Let's not do it, then. We'll both be happy."

Before Melissa could protest, Will turned and began to hobble off. And for a split second Melissa was so stung that she was going to let him just leave.

165

But then her anger boiled up inside her. *He's not going to get away with it*, Melissa thought bitterly. *He's not going to dump all of this on me.*

Melissa quickly stood. "Will," she hissed. He stopped in place and turned to look at her. "You're really going to bail?" she demanded, putting her hands on her hips. He opened his mouth as if to speak, but Melissa cut him off sharply. "You're really going to *not* plan the rally like your team is expecting you to?"

Will froze, looking like Melissa's words had the same effect as firing a shot at him would. For a long moment Will and Melissa just stood there in silence, glaring at each other. Melissa, for one, was not going to cave.

Then Will let out a frustrated, shaky sigh. "Fine," he muttered. He hobbled back toward Melissa's table. "But let's just get it over with."

"Okay, then," Melissa said, picking up her pen and pad of paper in a businesslike manner. "Let's begin with costumes."

And as Will sat himself down in the chair across from her, Melissa almost smiled.

Finally. She'd won a battle.

As Elizabeth stood in Conner's living room on Wednesday evening, she felt an eerie sense of déjà vu. The way that she and her friends—Tia, Maria, and Evan—were all waiting around for Conner to show up, anxious anticipation palpable in the air, seemed achingly similar to the time that they'd gathered to confront Conner for his intervention. *Too* similar.

And that was a night she had wanted to forget.

Elizabeth took a sip of ginger ale from the plastic cup she was holding. More than anything she just wanted to settle her nerves. Of course, many things about tonight were different from the way they'd been *that* night. For one, Tia had made a point of inviting people other than just Conner's close friends to this event, making for a bigger and less intense crew. But more important, of course, was that this was a *party*, not an intervention. It was a happy occasion. At least, it was supposed to be. Elizabeth chewed on the edge of her cup as she watched Jade stroll inside. The thing with Conner was that she never knew how he was going to react. And he could absolutely *hate* this surprise party.

He probably will, Elizabeth thought, releasing the cup from her gnawing teeth. But if Elizabeth was honest with herself, she had to admit that Conner's reaction to the party wasn't what was worrying her. It was Conner's reaction to *her*. Elizabeth placed her half-filled cup down on the tall bookshelf she was standing next to, wondering for the thirtieth time that day if she should have even come tonight.

"He's supposed to be here any minute," Jessica said, stepping up next to her.

Elizabeth glanced down at her watch and saw that her sister was right. Which meant there was no way Elizabeth could back out of this now.

"Liz? You okay?" Jessica asked, placing a comforting hand on Elizabeth's shoulder.

"Yes." Elizabeth forced a smile. With all of the smile forcing she'd been doing these past few days, she was becoming a real pro. "I'm fine."

Jessica opened her mouth to say something more, but at that moment Tia yelled out, "Okay, everyone, they're on their way!"

Lights were quickly shut off and everyone scurried about, moving out of direct view of the front door and window. Elizabeth found herself crouching behind the front-hall stairs, next to Evan and Jade.

"You think he's going to be mad?" Evan whispered to Elizabeth.

If Elizabeth hadn't been so anxious, she would have laughed. Everyone was so nervous about how the guest of honor was going to react to his surprise party that it suddenly seemed more than ridiculous that they were even bothering to throw him one. She shrugged. "Your guess is as good as mine."

Somebody—probably Tia—made a shushing noise, and everyone quickly quieted down. A second later there was the unmistakable sound of a key jiggling in a lock, strangely amplified in contrast to the silent house. Elizabeth's heart was beating so fast as she peeked around the staircase that it seemed like *she* was the one waiting to be surprised.

The front door swung open, and Elizabeth jumped up. "Surprise!" she yelled with everyone else as the lights were switched back on.

Conner, who had walked in with Andy, was visibly stunned. For a moment he just stood there, his green eyes frozen and wide like those of a deer caught in headlights, his body noticeably stiff.

Then, finally moving, Conner brought a hand up to his scruffy brown hair and glanced around the house. It must have been strange for him to realize that everyone present was staring at him. "What— What's this for?" he asked, his face paling. Again Elizabeth flashed back to the last time they'd been here like this, and she felt a pang of fear that Conner would see this as some kind of sick joke.

"Welcome home!" Tia blurted out. She ran over and gave him a big hug.

"You're not annoyed, are you?" she asked as she pulled back.

Conner raised his eyebrows, scanning the house once more. "Huh? Um, no." He focused on the group hanging out in the living room, stuffing a hand into his front jeans pocket. "It's a little . . . weird . . . , but I'm glad my friends are here." Conner glanced down at his work boots, his cheeks flushing. "You know. Still," he mumbled.

Elizabeth was standing close enough to hear Conner's words, but she couldn't help questioning if she heard them *right*. To say something like that, to actually admit that he was grateful for his friends' support and happy he hadn't lost it after everything that had happened—that was completely unlike the Conner she knew.

Conner glanced back up, and this time as he looked around, he noticed Elizabeth, his eyes resting on her for a moment.

Elizabeth's pulse raced as she locked eyes with Conner's, his gaze intense and penetrating. *Is he grateful that I'm still his friend?* she wondered. And then, despite her better instincts, Elizabeth allowed herself to wonder one more thing as Conner finally looked away from her.

Does he wish I was still his girlfriend?

Elizabeth bit her lip as her other friends walked over to greet Conner. She didn't know if she'd ever find out the answer to that one. But she did know one thing for sure, finally—*she* wished she was still his girlfriend.

"Here's my idea," Melissa said to Will, tapping her sleek silver pen against her pad of paper. "At the end of the rally the whole football team dances

170

around with the cheerleaders. It would be funny, and the crowd might really get into it." She put down the pen and picked up her mug of skim latte, finishing off the last drops. "So? Would the team do it?"

Will sat across from Melissa, barely hiding his annoyance. He simply couldn't stand the fact that Melissa had come up with a good suggestion. Actually, she'd come up with plenty of good suggestions tonight, although Will had argued against most of them purely out of spite, just to make Melissa's life more difficult. But it was pointless to fight her any longer. The girl was a master planner. She could get paid to do this kind of stuff.

Will crumpled up his napkin and tossed it into the garbage can to the right of Melissa's head. The thing that was truly bothering Will at the moment, however, wasn't Melissa's suggestions. It was the fact that as he sat so close to her for such an extended period and was forced to look right into her impossibly large, light blue eyes, Will was brought back to the past. The happy, before-the-injury past. When Melissa had been one of the most—if not *the* most—important aspects of his life.

Don't even start to go there, Will warned himself, looking down at the table. *Don't think of Melissa as your old girlfriend. Think of her as an old habit. An old, bad habit that you never want to fall into again.*

Will glanced back up, but he didn't quite meet

Melissa's eyes. "Sure, whatever. I think the team would do it. But they'll probably want to pick the song. They're not going to go for anything cheesy."

"Well, I don't think we'd *choose* anything cheesy, but fine," Melissa responded. She lifted her pen again, scribbling down some notes. "You can ask the team to vote on a song tomorrow at practice. Okay?"

Will simply shrugged. "Yeah. Fine." Leaning forward, he took a glance at Melissa's extensive notes. In the short time they'd been here, they seemed to have come up with a pretty detailed game plan. Most of this was due to Melissa, but Will was finished with trying to knock down her suggestions. Now he just wanted to get out of here—and away from her.

"We done?" he asked. "I mean, it looks like the thing's pretty much planned."

Melissa glanced up from the pad of paper, soft waves of her dark brown hair falling against her cheekbones. "I guess. I can type this all up for us at home and give it to Coach Laufeld tomorrow. Okay with you?"

Will swallowed. How was it that Melissa was always so together when it came to things like this? Why did she always know exactly what to do?

Right. The way she knew exactly how to stab me in the back and destroy my life, Will thought, his head starting to throb. He really was going to kill Ken. This whole situation was totally messing with his mind.

"Whatever, Melissa. Do what you want to do," Will said. He reached out for his crutches, scrambling to get up so he could leave already, and leaned his weight against them. But as Will stood, his left crutch slipped away and crashed down to the floor. Suddenly unbalanced, Will felt himself tipping . . . and about to fall.

Just as Will was shutting his eyes, bracing himself for the inevitable, he felt two arms rush behind him, supporting his back and preventing the fall.

"God, you scared me," Melissa said, her breath against his cheek. He swallowed, trying not to feel the sensations that were rushing through him at being so close to her.

After a second she stepped back, bending down to pick Will's left crutch off the floor as he rebalanced himself on his right one.

"Are you all right?" Melissa asked, handing Will the wooden support.

"Um, yeah," he managed to say. He cleared his throat, avoiding her gaze. How could she still affect him like this, after everything she'd done to him? The sound of her voice, the way she reached out for him out of pure instinct, helping him the way they'd always helped each other . . .

Don't forget she's an old habit, a voice in Will's brain piped up. *An old, bad habit.*

But then again, maybe it was true what they said about old habits—they really did die hard.

Conner glanced around his living room, taking in all of the people who were there—hanging out, talking, eating. Some were his close friends, some weren't, and Conner was amazed that he was actually enjoying himself. Tia had been the only one to proclaim this to be a "welcome-home" event. Everyone else seemed content to just chill and have a good time, not needing to make Conner the center of attention. Which was more than fine with him.

Conner spotted Megan's two best friends, Wendy and Shira, sitting cross-legged on the floor in the corner of the room. The sophomore girls were doing a very poor job of not making it obvious that they were staring at him.

Conner looked away from the girls. Some things never changed. And as Conner turned around and stared out the front window, he realized that this was the very reason that he found this party somewhat comforting. Coming home from rehab, Conner had felt like a total loner—even more so than usual. He knew that he had been anything but fun to be around before leaving, and he was worried that his friends would still be angry with him. Basically, he'd thought that he'd come home to find that his friends had disappeared.

But this party, corny as it was, showed Conner that his friends were still there for him. Jeff, Conner's rehab counselor, had drilled it into Conner's head enough times for Conner to realize that this was the kind of thing to be grateful for. And he was.

Taking a sip of Coke from the plastic cup in his hand, Conner ambled over to the couch, where Tia, Andy, Evan, and Jade were laughing about something—most likely Andy and Tia's recent stint on that crazy game show. Conner dropped down onto the narrow armrest next to where Tia was sitting. He watched everyone talk, but he wasn't really listening to what they were saying.

All he could think about was Elizabeth. And the fact that she was here. What did that mean? That she still wanted to be friends with him . . . or something more? Conner had no clue. Especially because he hadn't spoken to her at all. Conner couldn't even tell if he was avoiding her or if she was avoiding him. It seemed to be a mutual thing. As if they were both afraid what would happen when they came face-to-face.

Tia slapped Conner's knee, giggling hysterically. "Conner, you *have* to hear this story," she told him, her dark eyes teary from laughing so hard.

But Conner was too wound up to sit still. "In a sec," he said, standing. "Let me get a refill on my Coke."

As he walked away, Conner suddenly wished this

party was over. Now that his thoughts were all tangled up in Elizabeth, Conner wasn't in the mood for small talk.

Running a hand through his short, brown hair, Conner stepped into the kitchen . . . and saw Elizabeth standing there. Her back was to him, and she was emptying out her cup in the sink. She was the only person in the room.

For a split second Conner just took Elizabeth in—her silky blond hair, her slim frame. The profile of her delicate nose, the sexy curve of her neck.

Then Elizabeth turned around, spotting Conner before he could duck out and avoid her altogether. But it didn't matter. Avoiding Elizabeth was the last thing on Conner's mind at the moment.

"Hi," Elizabeth said, gripping the edge of the wooden counter.

"Hey," Conner returned, walking over to her. His pulse sped up as he neared Elizabeth and saw the vulnerable glint in her blue-green eyes, smelled the slightly floral scent of her perfume.

Elizabeth's full lips parted, as if she was about to say something, but no words came out.

"Thanks," Conner said gruffly.

Elizabeth shook her head, her luminous hair swinging from side to side. She glanced down at the yellow tiled floor. "Don't. I almost didn't come. I almost didn't—"

176

"I'm not thanking you for coming," Conner interrupted.

Elizabeth looked back up at him, her eyes wide and full of surprise.

"Thank you . . . for helping me." As Conner said the words, he felt a huge weight being lifted off his shoulders. He'd wanted to tell her that for so long. Finally he'd mustered up the guts. "For making me deal," he went on, kicking at the floor. Now that he'd started, he had to finish this thing. And it wasn't easy.

"When I was up in Red Bluff with my dad and going through all that stuff, I kept hearing your voice—your voice and my mom's." Conner let out a heavy breath, but he kept his eyes trained right on Elizabeth's. "You're the one who really got through to me. The only one."

Elizabeth bit her lip, her eyes starting to water. "Conner, I—" She shook her head, her voice cracking. "I thought you hated me."

Conner's heart felt like it was being wrenched apart. When he realized all that he'd put Elizabeth—one of the most incredible people in the world—through . . .

A tightness forming in his throat, Conner pushed a strand of Elizabeth's blond hair away from her eyes, then held his hand against her soft, warm cheek. His breath caught in his throat. "Liz. I could never hate you."

Elizabeth reached up and grasped his arm, and—almost as instinct—Conner pulled her toward him, cradling the back of her head with his hand. Without another thought Conner kissed Elizabeth, his heart pounding in his rib cage and his entire body heating up as he tasted her soft lips.

For a moment Conner lost himself in that kiss—a kiss that was sweet and sexy and familiar. A kiss that tasted like home. Conner never wanted to leave. He could kiss Elizabeth for days.

"Conner?"

Reality came rushing back, and every single muscle of Conner's tensed up at the sound of an achingly familiar female voice. Pulling away from Elizabeth, Conner hesitated for a moment before looking at the source of the voice, before acknowledging the fact that everything around him was going to come crashing down in a millisecond.

Then he looked.

And saw Alanna.

ELIZABETH WAKEFIELD

9:16 P.M.

Who is this girl? Why is she looking at Conner like that?

ALANNA FELDMAN

9:16 P.M.

Oh, no. It's Liz. She has to be.

CONNER MCDERMOTT

9:17 P.M.

Oh, man. Alanna . . . Liz . . . Alanna . . . this is bad.

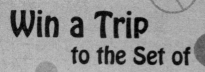